# DON'T LET ME FALL

# DON'T LET ME FALL

*a*

*n o v e l l a*

## LAKESHIA POOLE

*Don't Let Me Fall*
ISBN: 978-0-9910708-0-0
Second Edition
© 2012 by Lakeshia Poole
www.LakeshiaPoole.com

Published by Jack of All Trades Media LLC

Cover Design by: Brittani Roberts
Photo of young woman © Plush Studios / iStock by Getty Images

CHAPTER ONE | *Ciara*

Trey 1:21 AM
*Pick me up. Pls...now @5 qtr i druunk*

Ciara stared blankly at the text message of letters that did not belong together.

She'd planned to get as much rest as possible leading up to the first day of classes, but it looked like another night of her boyfriend Trey partying too much and her coming to his rescue. It was his friend Nate's 21st birthday and they had to go out and celebrate at exactly midnight.

When she didn't respond immediately, her phone buzzed and glowed blue as a reminder: *He needs you.*

She closed her eyes, wishing she hadn't seen the message, that her lids could erase the image with one swipe. She lay there, crafting a lie for the moment he asked her why she never showed up.

"What message?" she could ask. Or, "You know I don't get a signal on my phone in the Village."

Even under the cloud of *druunk*, Trey would spot her lie. He claimed the tip of her nose moved and her eyes went left automatically whenever she was dishonest.

The truth that she was still on edge after almost getting into a physical fight with her roommate Tala would not be a good enough reason.

In the two weeks since the girls began sharing the small space, they argued about any and every thing. The four white cinder block walls closed in tighter each day. Ciara's sticky note requests for Tala to clean up her side of the room evolved into disagreements over a too-loud TV and three a.m. XXX phone conversations.

After the shouting match over Tala 'borrowing' printer paper without asking, their resident advisor Kym pulled together a Kumbayah session. No one expected for them to become best friends, but respect was required.

Today they pushed respect aside and each other around after Ciara confronted her about golden condom wrappers left behind on her futon like little medals of honor.

Kym broke up the battle before blood was drawn, but Ciara knew the war was not over. This was just the beginning. The fire flushing Tala's face and her dark eyes solidified it— she had no intentions of making it work.

Ciara also knew that roommate drama would not be a valid reason for dismissing the love of her life.

For the past year she and Trey complained about their long-distance relationship—the high cell phone bills and weekend getaways that lasted as long as it took to get to each other.

*Once I get there things will get better.*

*Once we're together, it will all work out.*

When the time finally came, life moved so fast and they were always passing each other.

She couldn't *not* be there for Trey—even at 1:30 a.m.

Ciara squinted at her reflection in the full-body mirror hanging from the door. The gray Aurbor Grove University shorts and thin tank top she slept in would have to be good enough. She pulled the chestnut brown strands stroking her shoulders into a messy bun.

Keys in hand, she stumbled on one of Tala's wedge heels. "*Shhhhoot*...you've got to be kidding me."

She picked up the purple and hot pink shoe, dangling it over the trash can—destroying the self-professed shoe freak's beloved heels would take the war to another level and put Ciara on top.

Instead, she tossed it to Tala's side of the room and it rolled into her black mini-fridge.

When she opened the door, the sliver of fluorescent light from the hallway cast a spotlight onto Tala's empty bed, topped with a mound of clean and dirty clothes.

Ciara wasn't surprised that she hadn't returned. Outside of their fights, Tala was rarely there—usually hanging out late or staying at her parents' house in Aurbor Grove.

*Maybe she went home for good.*

Ciara hoped she never came back—the peace of having the room to herself felt good.

CHAPTER TWO | *Ciara*

It was a well-known fact that AGU was a party school, but it still surprised Ciara to see so many people filling the streets on a Wednesday night.

Downtown Aurbor Grove was a long island of bars and restaurants offering 24-7 happy hours and boutiques that didn't fit within the average college student's budget.

All of the debauchery happened between city government buildings and AGU's administrative offices.

After driving through the one-way streets several times, nearly running into a few stumbling pedestrians, she finally found a parking space.

The shrill voices of students, loud music and the smell of hotdogs sizzling at the corner-stand reminded her of the state fair.

She fell in stride behind a group of girls, heels click-clacking up Main Street's steep hill. They drunkenly shouted *"Go Wolves Go"* at random people. Their endless giggles and flirting with even drunker guys that asked them to kiss each other amused Ciara.

The closer she walked towards the heart of Downtown, the stronger the stench of the paper mill mixed with beer and liquor invaded her nose.

Rihanna's island-infused "Rude Boy" from Fifth Quarter and its neighbor's classic rock demand to "Pour Some Sugar On Me" came together in an unintended mash-up song. Not only did the two bars have vastly different playlists, but Fifth Quarter's sports bar theme of AGU helmets, green turf floor and rows of big-screen TVs presented a more modern, upscale look that stood out on the strip of bars.

Trey and his friends huddled on the patio around a black, wrought iron table littered with empty beer bottles and plastic cups.

Shot glasses overflowing with amber tequila clinked together with a toast of Happy Birthday to Nate. The trio tossed their heads back and reacted to the aftermath at the same time.

The lone girl raised her arms in a cheer and shimmied. "Whoo!"

Nate chased his with a long swig from his Miller High Life beer. "Man that burns!"

Trey scrunched his face reddened by the summer heat that didn't let up at night. His big Will Smith ears were especially full of color.

Ciara reached out and tugged on his shirt.

"Oh, hey baby, you came!" Trey's hazel eyes were small slits and his smile wide.

"You texted me, remember?"

"Mm-hmm." He danced and played with a thin red straw, working it in and out of the gap between his two front teeth. "Check me out."

She watched him do a little two-step and couldn't help but laugh. His silliness doubled when he was tipsy. A blue blob stained the embroidered polo player on his gold Ralph Lauren shirt—evidence that it had been a real good night.

15

Ciara kept her eyes on Trey's performance but noticed the girl. She didn't say hello or even acknowledge Ciara's presence.

In her own tequila-hazed world, she mimicked Rihanna's winding and grinding.

Tendrils fell over her face, leaving only plump glossy lips. Hair and lips. She could have been the pretty sister of the smoking piano man from John Bua's print hanging on Ciara's wall.

Was she with them or just passing by for the free alcohol?

"I thought you wanted a ride home. It looks like you guys are still celebrating."

"Your boy was late, so we had to make up for lost time. Go hard or go home," Nate yelled over the music, bouncing his shoulders. That shot had begun to work its magic.

"I see," Ciara said. She had drunk some punch and a couple bottles of Smirnoff before, but she didn't understand the allure of hard liquor. It burned, tasted horrible, and made people act like this. Why would she want something that caused her to lose control and become a totally different person?

Trey jumped over the ledge and onto Ciara, making her stumble into a group of girls dancing on the sidewalk.

"My sweet CC." He ran his palm down her broad forehead, cupping her high cheekbones.

"You are so good to me. I got the best girl, don't I Nate?"

"Yeah, you're a real lucky dude."

"Are you ready to go?" she asked, holding on to him.

"I guess we better call it a night."

"I'll help you get him to the car," Nate said.

It took both of them to hoist him in the passenger seat.

"Thanks for making sure he didn't end up arrested or in the drunk tank again."

Nate lingered at her open driver's door.

"Well, have a good night," she yawned.

He stepped in the opening before she could close the door. "Hey, could you maybe give me and Maya a ride to Simpson Hall?"

"You and who?"

"Oh, I thought you knew her," he mumbled, pointing a thumb over his shoulder. "She was at the bar with us."

She watched Maya's long, shapely legs move down the hill, her curls wild, her white mini-skirt swishing from side-to-side. Hair. Lips. Legs.

"We would walk but South campus is so far."

"Sure. Get in."

Trey flipped through the radio dial, finally landing on a station pounding out bass-filled party songs that he could rap along to.

"Don't I know you from somewhere?" Maya slurred.

Her thick Southern accent made her sound sultry, instead of sloppy. It didn't seem like a voice so husky was meant to come out of those lips.

"I don't think so," Ciara said, staring back in the rearview mirror.

"I guess you have one of them familiar faces."

"Are ya'll hungry?" Trey asked.

Ciara pointed to the dashboard. "No. It's after two o'clock in the morning."

"We could just pull up to Mickey D's right quick. It's open 24 hours."

"That's not the point. I'm tired."

"Well, I'm starving. I need something to soak up all this liquor."

"I wouldn't mind having some fries, myself," Nate said, rubbing his stomach.

Ciara took a deep breath, pressed down the words that popped up because she knew they would lead to another embarrassing argument.

She was tired of all the fighting.

She made an ugly, screeching U-turn on Main Street and headed towards the golden arches.

The long line crawled forward and by the time she made it to the intercom, Trey snored softly and she placed his usual order.

He didn't wake up until Nate slammed the door.

"Appreciate the ride, CC."

Trey leaned out the window. "Ya'll have a good night."

Ciara drove slowly around the drop-off circle.

"So that's Maya?"

"That's Maya."

"Miami Maya?"

"Yes. That's the Maya that went to Miami with us."

19

They were both quiet at the abnormally long red light. Ciara watched the bright orange crosswalk timer count down, but the light still didn't change.

"I didn't know she was hanging out with you tonight."

"I mean, she and Nate work together." He dug for the french-fries at the bottom of the white bag. "It's his choice to bring whoever he wants to celebrate his birthday."

"But don't you think it's weird that a girl hangs out with ya'll like that?"

Trey laughed, his mouth half-full. "I cannot believe you're really gonna interrogate me right now."

"Please don't yell at me."

"You've got to get over your insecurity issues," he said, shaking his head.

"Don't try to flip this on me. I'm not being insecure. I asked you a simple question." She stared straight ahead, knowing that he would just give her that look; the scowl that made her feel like she was overreacting, like she was crazy.

"No, you're not just asking a question."

She raised her voice an octave higher. "Why are you avoiding my question? That's what I want to know."

He pressed the unlock button and turned to her.

They were so close, yet so far apart.

"I'll walk." He grabbed the bag and unbuckled his seatbelt in one swift move.

*Is he for real?*

"Trey come back!" Her plea hit his back as he strolled in the direction of Simpson Hall...and Maya.

Finally the light turned green.

## Chapter Three | *Ciara*

Ciara drove all the way to the top of The Village parking deck to find a space. The radio station transitioned to slow R&B songs about love. How ironic.

She clicked the engine off and sat in the stillness of her car, replaying the night, wondering what she could have done differently. Maybe she shouldn't have said anything. She could have waited to ask him about Maya when he was sober.

Brightness emanated from the teal numbers on the dashboard. 3:10 AM. She watched until they blinked to 3:18, thinking about Maya—so confident, dark and beautiful.

*Is he with her right now?*

Ciara caught a glimpse of herself in the rearview mirror. Her downturned lips and puffy eyes showed just how tired she'd become. Not just from being awakened to rescue Trey, but of their relationship. Here she was nitpicking her own features, wondering if he preferred Maya's thickness to her slender frame; her wild and curly tresses to Ciara's simple ponytail. Her voice that oozed sensuality and sounded like she should sing the blues.

She wiped away tears with her thumbs, her throat hurting from the ones she held back. She never imagined her college years kicking off like this. With all the crazy thoughts running through her mind, she doubted she'd get any sleep, but headed to the dorm anyway.

"I'm sorry you can't go in this entrance," a campus officer said, holding up her palms.

"Why not?" Ciara asked with irritation that made the lanky officer purse her lips.

"If you could, please wait in the courtyard with the other residents."

At first, Ciara lingered in the back alongside hundreds of other agitated residents complaining about how they were ready to crawl back to bed for a few more hours of sleep.

*Why would they have a fire drill? Tomorrow is the first day of class after all.*

Some, however, were morbidly curious, sharing their questions and theories aloud.

*Is that a body?*

*Why did the police car pull off so fast?*

*Why are they questioning him?*

*Who would do something like this?*

Caldwell Hall loomed over them all, casting its own judgment. Yellow square windows were lit throughout all 10 floors, creating an ominous halo above The Village courtyard.

Curiosity pulled her through the crowd. She pushed between the weary students dressed in an eclectic mix of pajamas and partygoers donning spaghetti-strapped dresses and heels.

"Excuse me. Sorry."

Earlier that day the grassy knoll connecting all four residence halls buzzed with the mix of excitement and anxiety that comes with the start of a new semester.

Now resident advisors passing out free pizza had been replaced with police officers and emergency officials ordering students to get back.

President Gilmore looked like he'd never made it home, dressed in a dark navy suit, his silver hair slicked across a shiny, bald cul-de-sac. He paced around looking serious and official, hands linked behind his back.

That's when she saw it. The blood.

It seeped into the hard, Georgia clay, staining the blades of grass with a crimson tint that matched the garden's roses.

Tour guides said that Lorena Caldwell—the wife of the dormitory's namesake—loved red roses. So much so, that her husband guaranteed the University his contribution to its endowment as long as Lorena's garden lived on.

Urban legends had a different twist on the story claiming it as Lorena's final resting place, forever adorned with her favorite flower.

This incident would add another spin for the tale.

"They probably got us out here because they didn't want anybody to see what really went down," she overheard a guy say.

"What happened?" she asked.

Ciara's voice pulled his eyes to hers, big and full of a fear that made him stumble over his words.

"T-Tala jumped and she, uh, she...killed herself."

## Chapter Four | *Nick*

"Who are you?"

Professor Garrett leaned on the silver edge of the desk, running his hand through thick, graying-brown hair. He watched his newest batch of students shift uncomfortably in the hard-back chairs and smirked.

"And what the hell are you doing in my classroom?" Several open-mouth gasps livened up the stark, white room.

"I imagine you came here thinking, 'Freshman seminar will be an easy A,' right?" A few students boldly chuckled along with him. He crossed his arms and began pacing the gray carpet. "No, seriously, tell me what this class is all about. In your own words."

Nick glanced around the U-shaped auditorium as hands rose tentatively. There was an Asian guy and two girls who shared his brown-hued skin tone. He had been the solo minority in Art History, so this was diverse comparatively.

The last stats he'd seen, only 1.5% of AGU students were Black men. This was obvious when he came on the campus tour last Fall, but actually living in a 98.5% world was an adjustment and required a great sense of humor.

When a guy in his orientation group probed him about what it felt like to play on the football team, it flattered him because he had been trying to bulk up. He shrugged it off when he realized the guy thought that athleticism was the only way he could get into AGU. But the affirmative action 'joke' that followed had him ready to fight.

Nick never knew being a minority could make him *feel* so minor. He should have been ready for this feeling, this overwhelming awareness of being different. So many people warned him about the campus' history, the study hard-party harder culture, and the fact that there would be few diverse faces. The truth was he didn't believe them. None of his close relatives had even finished a semester at the technical college.

What did they know about attending one of the top universities in the country?

"For the most part, you all have an idea of what we're doing here. Fresh Start is a bridge program," Professor Garrett said. "It's one way we help freshmen get acclimated to the college workload. You know, we let you move in early to get your bearings, but know that throughout the summer session, there will be no handholding. Yes, I take attendance–and I expect you to be on time. Do the work and you'll get your easy A."

Professor Garrett reviewed the course syllabus, required books, upcoming tests and papers, reading over his glasses in a monotonous voice. It didn't sound like an easy A to Nick. If it hadn't been a required course, he would've dropped it.

"So back to what I asked earlier. Who are you and what are you doing in my classroom?"

He walked up the stairs passing out fluorescent colored index cards to each row.

Nick focused on perfecting the masterpiece doodle of the cockatoo-nosed girl in front of him. When Professor Garrett came to his row, he removed his rimless glasses and gawked at the image.

"Nice to see you're off to a good start, Mr.?"

Nick hesitated, tapping his pen on the desk. This was not the first impression he wanted to make, but everyone stared at him for a response. "Barclay."

Professor Garrett kept walking, satisfied with the humiliation he caused.

"So I need each of you to write down your name, hometown, major, career goal and one thing you expect to learn from the Fresh Start program."

Nick scribbled hurriedly, watching as others dropped their cards on Professor Garrett's desk. He reread his answers, sighing at the fragment and run-on sentences, tempted to correct them but not wanting the professor to see the obvious uncertainty in his erasure marks.

He'd been asked the questions before: Who are you? Where are you from? What are your career goals? Each time he answered he felt like a phony perpetrating as one of the eager beaver students that surrounded him. He wasn't sure how he ended up here. While he had been expected to go to college, he hadn't been groomed to be the next generation AGU grad like many of his classmates.

Nick smiled and spoke deliberately, trying hard to conceal the dialect of his Southern tongue.

He learned the school chants, cheering louder and prouder than anyone because in fact it did feel great to belong to the AGU Wolf Pack. To be somewhere other than Sandersville. To not be just some poor kid from the country abandoned by both mother and father. To no longer be called the Black guy with the high SAT score who 'acted White.'

Nope, he wasn't known as the band geek whose only interaction with popular cheerleaders was passing them on his way to the half-time performance—not anymore.

No, here Nick Barclay could be whoever and whatever he chose to be.

## CHAPTER FIVE | *Nick*

Nick spotted the two Black girls from Professor Garrett's seminar talking outside the classroom. While everyone else rushed out, he waited around, catching the end of their conversation.

"I can't believe he includes attending social outings in our grade," said the thinner one with the same complexion as the mocha iced coffee in her hand.

"I can tell right now he's going to be a handful."

"Sorry to interrupt, but aren't ya'll in my Fresh Start seminar?"

He reached out, a tattoo of the name 'Cynthia' permanently intertwined with the forearm veins leading to his heart. "I'm Nick."

"Mr. Barclay, right?"

His faced warmed with the same awkwardness he felt when Professor Garrett initially called him out. "I see you were paying attention."

"Faraji." She offered one small hand, the fingers of her other massaging the pearls drooping around her neck. "And this is Ciara."

They began to walk and he followed.

"You know I would really appreciate it if you both sat behind me next week."

Faraji shifted her weight to the left as if preparing to attack.

"I know you're not trying to say my head is too big for you to see?" she asked, smoothing her hand across the sleek copper ponytail. "And if that's the case *move...closer.*"

"Nah, that's not even it. I'm just saying you two beautiful ladies had my attention the whole time. That kinda distraction might make me fail and we can't have that."

A warm 'I can't believe this guy' expression came over Faraji's heart-shaped face. God's natural blush of cinnamon-red freckles rounded out her raised cheeks.

"Corny, but funny."

"Do you always approach women like that?" Ciara asked.

"I figured flattery mixed in with a little comedy might be the best way to break the ice," he said. "Are ya'll sisters?"

The two of them laughed—the way their curvaceous lips spread into a smile the same way confirmed it.

"No," Faraji said. "We both live in Caldwell."

"Oh, cool, I'm across the yard in Roskill. So did you get the books for that class yet?"

"I was actually about to go pick them up now. I'm so last minute," Faraji said.

"I checked them out in the bookstore and the used ones add up to like $150."

"Are you for real?"

"Dead serious. Who wants to pay that kinda money for books we'll never use again? The professor wrote one of 'em. I think dude's trying to up his book sales."

"Dr. Garrett's a pretty well-respected expert in the field of youth crime and subculture," Ciara spoke over them.

Both Faraji and Nick frowned.

"So, I did a little research," she said defensively, jiggling the ice against the plastic cup.

"I wanted to see if ya'll wanted to go in on the books? Split the cost three ways and share."

"I can't believe you came over here to hustle books out of us because we're the only other Black people in the class," Ciara snapped.

"It's not like that. We can rotate or meet up and review the chapters together. My roommate's sharing with his classmates to save money."

"I know I don't have that much money for nobody right now," Faraji said. "You would think with the amount they're charging for this program, books would be included."

"I know right." Nick grinned at Ciara, hoping to melt away the icy wall she'd built up. "Won't be no hard feelings if you don't want to, but I'll pick them up tonight if ya'll are down."

"Maybe," she muttered.

"Speaking of tonight, are ya'll going to the Theta party?" Faraji asked.

"What party?"

"It's a Thursday."

Nick and Ciara spoke simultaneously, making him laugh at their obvious dissimilarities. He tried to hide his attraction to the innocence in her eyes, the natural pout of her lips.

Faraji pulled a red handbill from her purse and read the information. "It's at some club called Inferno."

"Did you see that syllabus? We have a quiz first thing next week," Ciara said, sounding stressed already.

"Come on, it's the first party of the semester," Faraji pressed.

"I'm not really into parties anyway."

"Goin' to a party school has a way of changing that," Nick said.

Ciara paused, looking away, searching for an excuse he assumed.

"If I can find something to wear." She began walking backwards towards the approaching shuttle. "I have a meeting, so I have to catch this bus. See you later?"

"Alright, girl." Faraji waved and Nick watched her, curly hair bouncing over her shoulders.

"Oh, I wouldn't go there, Nick. You know that's the girl they say killed her roommate."

CHAPTER SIX | *Ciara*

When the shuttle bypassed The Village, Ciara glared at its tall brick buildings. Students scattered across the courtyard, off to class, leaving the dining hall, or chatting with friends. Things were back to 'normal,' but she felt stuck in the madness of last night.

Throughout the day she experienced these moments, not blackouts, but the feeling that she was standing outside of herself watching life happen.

She hadn't slept, relying on coffee and energy shots to keep her from crashing.

When her mother Carolyn showed up to take her home to recuperate for a few days, she rejected that as a solution. She didn't want to run away or allow this tragedy to mar her first semester.

*Maybe you shouldn't go to class tomorrow*, Carolyn suggested, but Ciara wasn't hearing it. She wanted to move forward with life as planned, even if everything appeared out of control.

Carolyn's answer was lots of prayer...and questions. She wanted to know everything about Tala and Ciara wasn't ready to tell the full truth about their constant battles.

It felt good to have her mother at her side, but she needed to convince Carolyn to leave and let her be. She wanted her to trust and believe that she could overcome this—as an adult, not some wimpy child.

Ciara got off the shuttle and walked a couple blocks North to The Royal Peacock hotel.

She marveled at how different Downtown looked and smelled during the daytime. No raucous music or girls dancing in the street. Everyone walked like they had somewhere to be.

The only consistent characteristic was how May's humidity created a dewy sheen of perspiration on her skin— morning, noon and night.

People rolling endless black bags checked in and out of the busy lobby. She didn't have the patience for the elevator, skipping up the stairs to the third floor.

She fed the plastic room key into the slot, but Carolyn had the door dead-bolted.

"It's me, your daughter."

"Hold on a second." Carolyn slid and clicked all the locks and opened the door. "There you are."

"I just got out of my freshman seminar," Ciara said, sitting on the disheveled queen-sized bed.

Her mother continued work away from the office with file folders, spreadsheets and a red-blinking Blackberry laid out across the down comforter.

She admired how Carolyn's sleeveless sky blue maxi dress showed off her curves, but knew her narrow frame wouldn't fill it out as well. Carolyn was a young mother and proud of it. She blurred the line of friend and mother often, because it had been just the two of them for most of Ciara's life.

"So how was it?" Carolyn beamed, plopping down next to her.

"A little hectic. I have about six chapters of reading to do for Sociology before Friday and a quiz on Tuesday."

"Ohh, my poor baby," she moaned in a sorrowful tone. "I'm so sorry you have to deal with what happened and take on all this work."

Ciara sat still, letting her be needed. Nothing offended Carolyn more than *not* being needed.

"Did I tell you how much I like your hair down like that? I don't know when you had the time to put all those curls in there, but it's really pretty sweetie."

"Thank you." Ciara twirled the ringlets with her finger, let them fall over her forehead. "They're not as tight as I wanted but...I just felt like doing something different."

"Whatever makes you happy."

"I'm happy I have you here all to myself."

"Well, have you heard from Trey?"

"No."

"I don't know about him. How could he ignore you like that?"

Ciara pulled away and shook her head. "We got into a fight before..." She couldn't bring herself to even say Tala's name, let alone mention what happened.

"Maybe what you had in high school was just that. It sounds like you two are growing further apart."

"You don't understand."

"I'm sure I do. I was married once. And I've been in plenty of fights."

"But you and Daddy were different."

"Love is love. It ain't no different whether it's coming from you, him or me. It feels good and hurts just the same."

"I guess you could say that."

"I just don't want you to lose *you*, baby," Carolyn said softly. Her voice held remnants of pain and regret. "You're young. This is the best time in your life. Don't spend it chasing after a boy."

Ciara silently watched the news ticker scroll across the flat-screen TV.

"So when are you going back to Atlanta?"

"Now you're really trying to get rid of me, huh?" she laughed.

"I just don't want you missing out on work. I told you I'm fine."

"Trust me that office is not missing me." Carolyn gently grabbed her wrists, their matching silver bracelets clanging. "Are you sure you're gonna be okay?"

She gazed into the brown eyes that matched her very own, searching for deception in the gold speckles.

"Maybe," Ciara mumbled, lowering her head. "If you take me to get my nails done, I'll be real fine."

"Okay, that sounds like my daughter."

"See, I'm fine."

CHAPTER SEVEN | *Ciara*

Seven days after Tala's fall, Mr. Bing came to pick up her things. A petite man, Ciara stood almost half a foot taller than him and she could see the brown age spots dotting across his baldhead.

"How are you Mr. Bing?"

"I am okay. Thank you for asking."

He appeared a lot better than when Ciara offered her condolences at the AGU memorial service for Tala. The dark, crescent-shaped bags under his eyes had disappeared, but the sadness lingered.

"I packed up all of her stuff for you."

Ciara left Tala's side of the room empty and clean with the faint scent of lemon.

She pulled down Tala's Lil' Wayne, Nicki Minaj and Lady Gaga posters and folded them neatly atop her freshly washed sheets and towels. She washed her dirty clothes and tossed out the unsavory wardrobe pieces like her slinky dresses and explicit t-shirts reading 'I'm That B!*@^' and 'F U, Pay Me.'

She trashed her 'toy box' full of gels and gadgets that would surely make Mr. Bing's olive skin blush red.

Tala's Hello Kitty collection of pens, picture frames, pads, clock, her laptop and textbooks were sealed in boxes and labeled appropriately.

When she came to the hooker heels she often neglected at the entryway, Ciara thought about that night. When she'd wished the girl away, she didn't mean it.

Mr. Bing slowly loaded everything, carefully considering each box. Seeing Tala's brief life at AGU stacked up on a rusty dolly created a feeling of finality Ciara hadn't expected. She was really gone...forever.

"Thank you so much. I couldn't have sorted through it all without breaking down."

"It's the least I could do."

"In the short time that Tala knew you, she always say you were a nice girl."

"Really?" Ciara said, biting her bottom lip. Did he hear the shock in her tone? She recovered with, "That was sweet."

"You know it really was hard for us to send her off to school, even if only a few miles away. Me and my wife, we are always traveling for work. So it meant the world to us that she was able to make friends fast."

"Yes...she was a good person and I'll miss her," she said, darting her eyes left.

Mr. Bing sat on Tala's bare mattress. Ciara thought she should have offered him a seat on the futon. Those beds felt like slabs of concrete.

"I still can't believe that she would do something like this." Tears didn't come, but he frowned, taking deep breaths.

"Mr. Bing," Ciara said, knowing that no words she could offer him would be good enough. She told him what she chanted to herself. "It will be fine."

They weren't the only ones still in a state of disarray.

AGU had its ongoing investigation, particularly around how she gained access to the secure rooftop. Two residence hall staff members had been fired over that.

The school newspaper, *The Silver Bullet*, had been respectful, but speculated why the Presidential Scholar with the perfect SAT score on the cusp of a new life would end it all.

Ciara refused their interviews. They described her role in simple words with potential for suspicion: "The last person to see Tala Bing was her roommate Ciara Capers."

The articles asked why no one saw it coming. Were there any actions, words that could have potentially foreshadowed her leap?

A picture of Tala, surrounded by kids during a volunteer trip to her native Philippines accompanied the full-page spread. The caption explained that her name meant 'bright star' in Tagalog and she had been just that.

It also noted that in her AGU application essay, she wrote of pursuing medicine and opening a low-cost clinic in Aurbor Grove. She vowed to never leave her impoverished neighborhood behind.

In death, editors revised life to consist of only the scenes the person got right.

The piece didn't sound like the Tala she knew.

Not the Tala that woke up after noon and returned in the wee hours of the morning, gin evaporating from her skin.

Or the Tala that called her mother every possible derivative of the F word when she didn't deposit the money she wanted fast enough.

"I need to know for certain...what happen to my daughter." Mr. Bing sighed deeply.

"We hired a private investigator. He wants to ask you some questions. If you remember *anything* please share it with him."

*Would it really help to divulge Tala's wild ways?*

*It's obvious she lived bipolar lifestyles. It got to her and she felt she only had one way out of both of them.*

"I know there were times when you didn't get along." He held something back, the bulge in his throat bobbled up and down against his tight, leathery skin.

"We all make mistakes. But we can make up for that if we're honest."

She'd heard the vicious rumors, whispered behind her back.

Yes, they argued, but their disagreements never reached *that point.*

Yes, the police interviewed her as a witness, not a suspect. Their initial findings were clear: no foul play.

Ciara took a few steps towards the door to let him know that she was uncomfortable with where the conversation was going.

Her heart and voice in full defense mode, she said, "I told the police everything I know, Mr. Bing."

He stood up and rolled what was left of Tala Bing behind him.

"The cops have no idea what they're doing. They've barely spoken to us since she..." His mouth moved, but he couldn't bring himself to say the words, so he swallowed them. "If you could, just, please speak with the private investigator."

"I'll talk to him. Promise."

## Chapter Eight | *Ciara*

The next day she agreed to meet Trey in The Village courtyard. He looked as somber as Mr. Bing, sitting alone on the bench.

"Hey you." A smile flickered over his face, slightly red from the sun glaring over them. "Thanks for meeting with me."

They hugged and she pulled away first.

"You look pretty," he said, reaching out to touch the dark green sateen tunic.

"Thank you."

"I thought you got out of class earlier?"

"I had a meeting for freshman seminar. We have a team building exercise this weekend," Ciara said, not hiding her disdain.

She ran two fingers up her temple and pulled an invisible trigger on the throbbing pain caused by her classmate Laura Beth's bossy, nasally voice.

Ciara had grown to hate group work. Half the time her teammates talked about rushing and living in one of the plantation-style homes on Greek Row. The rest of the time they ignored her ideas like she was some alien that crash-landed at their school.

"I don't think I can take a weekend with Laura Beth."

"Oh, I'm sure you'll have fun."

"I don't know. I'm not like you, Mr. Popular."

He patted her head. "I could teach you some things my little freshman."

"What, like how to answer the phone? I haven't seen you in over a week." Her tone was calm, almost kind. The atmosphere between them changed nonetheless.

He looked around—people lounged on the lush green grass reading. A group of guys competed in a loud game of volleyball.

"Can we go to my room?"

She began to shake her head, before answering.

"I want to talk to you privately. Please."

"Okay."

Ciara wasn't supposed to give in so easily. She wanted to fight him, but she let him grab her hand as they hopped on the elevator.

A few residents complained about the rigor of summer session and made plans for the weekend.

Others talked about still being "freaked out" about the girl who killed herself.

"Whatever. I heard her crazy roommate lost it and pushed her," a guy claimed. "Seriously dude, I don't even walk through the courtyard no more. I swear the blood's still there."

Ciara stared straight ahead, feeling Trey's eyes fall on her. She flinched when he touched her shoulder—a gesture meant to comfort her. It didn't.

She swallowed the bitter mix of anger and embarrassment, then cleared her throat. She shrugged his hand away and lifted her head a little higher.

The doors separated with a jerk and the all-male floor's signature scents of popcorn and feet greeted Ciara.

She breathed through her mouth until inside his room—a spacious home by dorm standards.

As a Resident Advisor, Trey had the privilege of double the square footage and a private bathroom. Movie posters of Tony Montana gripping his 'little friend,' Leonides declaring 'This Is Sparta!' and 'The Godfather' petting his beloved cat hung from the walls.

He moved video game controllers and a stack of hardback business textbooks, clearing a space for her on the futon.

"Some people have to come up with their own theories. They can't comprehend suicide. I'm sorry about those dummies in the elevator."

"I'm fine. They're not the first idiots I've had to deal with. Probably won't be the last," she muttered.

"I have something for you." Before she could say anything, he snapped open a blue velvet box before her.

Her eyebrows creased, a smile played at her lips. "What's this for?"

"It's my promise that I'm going to do a better job taking care of you."

She held out her hand, admiring the glimmer of the deep red garnet jewels against the dull, artificial light. The cluster of bright gems and clear diamonds formed a rose.

He reached for her hand. "I read somewhere that garnet stones represent passion, truth, and courage."

"Oh, yeah. Where'd you get that from?"

"Google," he laughed. "You know they say stones have healing power."

"You would research something like that. I bet you know who mined the diamonds and everything."

She always joked about how he overanalyzed everything to death. He refused to buy anything without reading pages of reviews and doing a thorough cost comparison. It didn't matter that he could afford the best, he wanted to be sure he was getting the best always.

"Seriously, I wanted it to mean something. For you. For us."

"Aw. I love it. I really do." She kissed his cheek, leaving an imprint of her lipstick.

"I'm really proud of you starting school early. Most folks would take the regular route and chill out all summer."

"Well, you know the main reason I'm participating in this program, right?"

He shook his head, biting his lip. "Nah, tell me."

"Ugh, you and your ego."

"Okay, okay, okay. That's another reason why I'm happy. We get to be together. Finally."

"But are we? I feel like so much has changed since I got here. I need to know that we're on the same page."

He ran a thumb over her chin and planted soft kisses from her ear to her lips. "Yes. I love you. More than you'll ever know."

"That crap you pulled when I picked you up was not necessary. And then I tried to call you." She talked with her hands, the volume of her rant steadily increasing with each word, every motion.

"I heard nothing, *not one word,* from you. You say you love me, but why would you do something like that?"

"Hold up, calm down." He surrendered, raising both palms. "I'm sorry. I know I went overboard. I thought it was better if we had some space."

"I don't think you get it. I sat in that police station. By myself." She looked at him for a response.

When nothing came, she continued, "I was in there looking like a criminal. Now everybody thinks I killed her."

"CC, they're just stupid rumors. And didn't you say Miss Carolyn came down to be with you? I know she took care of everything."

"But I wanted *you* to be there for me. She had to drive over three hours. You were three minutes away." Her demeanor softened, all the vulnerabilities she had withheld seeping out.

"I need you to be honest with me."

"I am being honest."

One question was entangled in her thoughts since that night.

"Why do you get so defensive when I ask you about Maya?"

"Trust is the foundation. When you ask me about her, it reminds me that you don't trust me. Where there's no trust, there's no love."

She sat still and quiet.

"Maya's just a friend. She's not interested in me like that."

"How do you know? The ratio here is what, five to one? Every girl in The Village is probably interested in you."

"Not Maya."

"Why not?"

His voice fell low, as if it wasn't just the two of them in the room. "Because she's into girls, okay?"

Ciara's lips parted and her eyes widened.

"She's in a weird place right now about it. And as a friend, I promised to keep it a secret." He shrugged his bulky shoulders. "But I guess her secret isn't worth ruining what we have."

"Maya's a lesbian?"

"Yes."

"Wow." Ciara cleared her throat. "Well, she doesn't act gay."

"And how does a gay person act?" he asked sarcastically. "You sound real ignorant right now."

"I thought...I don't know what I think."

"You assumed."

After a long pause she finally acquiesced. "Yes, I assumed. I was wrong."

"Maya's a good person. I'm not going to treat her any differently because of that."

Ciara released all the pent up emotions in a long sigh. Rested her head on his shoulder. "I'm sorry."

"Me too. I should've come out with the truth. It would've saved us a lot of drama, arguing over nothing."

"I think I'm still sensitive after what happened last week."

"I can only imagine. I wish I could've been there for you."

"I saw her fall, you know." She whispered the confession so calmly, he moved from under her.

"What?"

"Tala. I saw her fall."

"When? How?"

"I dreamed about her. It was like she was trying to tell me something."

He laughed uneasily. "What, you were on some *Sixth Sense* type stuff?"

"No, I wasn't scared at all. It felt...peaceful."

Trey pulled her into his arms, pressed his lips against her forehead. "Are you alright?"

Ciara squeezed his arms tighter around her, the security of their love comforting like nothing else.

"I'm fine," she said.

But when she closed her eyes, Tala was on the rooftop, beckoning to her, enveloped by jet-black hair.

Maybe she did do something to cause Tala's death and would forever be haunted by it.

CHAPTER NINE | *Nick*

Nick found a study room with comfortable chairs and a long glass window perfect for people watching.

A week out from midterms, the stress of catching up with readings and reviewing notes from the past month descended upon them swiftly. The student center was packed, so the act of securing a room in the midst of that chaos was like successfully re-discovering American soil.

He tackled Art History and passed off Garrett's books to Faraji. Divide and conquer. It was quiet except for the sound of her creating a rainbow of yellow, pink and green highlighted text.

She claimed she had a system. Ciara swore by her color-coded note cards.

Nick flicked a pen between his fingers. Pierre-Auguste Renoir's *Girl with a Hoop* stared at him, but his eyes were drawn to the essay slaughtered with red slashes, tucked in the back of his textbook.

Maybe he needed a system or something.

He thought the professors had to be insane to expect him to memorize such a large amount of material. Sure he liked the fact that there was little-to-no homework, but having 80% of his grade come from two tests scared him.

Instead of the As he was accustomed to, he became awfully familiar with all the other letters plastered on his quizzes and papers. Each week made him wonder if.

*If I can't make it in Art...*

*If I drop out now, it's not like I've missed the whole summer.*

*If I get a job, I could make some real money...now.*

*If I have to go back...*

Going back to Sandersville was out of the question. He had always felt like a displaced person there.

His grandmother Lucille would not settle for anything less than a college degree *with honors*.

College had been a non-negotiable. Despite the fact that Lucille gained no more than a fourth grade education, she wanted him to know that the price had been paid; she'd attended during a time when Black children walked to school as White students zoomed by on busses, some pelting them with rocks.

Jesus and college. Those were two things she instilled into him at an early age. Both were deemed saviors that he needed to change his life.

The Fresh Start program was supposed to help him get used to the campus, the people and college life. If anything it stirred up questions, feelings, and thoughts he'd never considered, leaving him all mixed up on what to do next.

A group of beach-tanned girls with the same hair as Renoir's girl caught his attention. They laughed and talked their way to the front of the long, winding line at the JavaWorks Cafe.

Large plastic cups of iced coffee to ward off the June heat in one hand, books in the other, they were so carefree.

It seemed like they all had this college thing figured out.

He knew people—*smart people*—who went to college only to return divorced from their former self, dreams irretrievably broken.

They either assured him they were going back or muttered college ain't for everybody.

*What if it ain't for me?*

The expansive campus and student body made up of faces that did not resemble his, voices that didn't have the same twang made his inadequacies even more apparent. Sometimes being a member of the 1.5% made him feel like a new millennium version of Ralph Ellison's invisible man.

He'd flexed his best writing skills for the Art History essay, opening with an art quote from Mr. Ellison.

Professor Eidsvick skipped over his eloquent preface and went straight to marking up each comma splice and passive verb.

"Have ya'll done office hours with any of your professors yet?"

"No, but my Sociology professor is always complaining about how nobody shows up," Ciara said.

She licked her index finger and flipped through a thick course companion—a plastic coiled collection of articles and essays hand-picked by the professor and sold exclusively (and exorbitantly) at the campus printing shop.

"I wonder if I can get extra credit or something."

Faraji smirked. "Already? That'd be my last resort."

"Yeah, I don't know." He glared at the weird girl balancing the gold hoop with her foot. He didn't care about her or Renoir. He didn't get the significance or understand what he should offer as the right answer. "Guess I would feel stupid asking for something like that."

"Then again it's better than failing your first semester," Ciara said.

"True."

"And we wouldn't want you to leave us." The glance Faraji offered him was brief, but it was clear in the reflection of her dark irises that she wanted him.

How had he missed it before?

"What if I left?"

Ciara stood up, stretched her fingertips upward. "You better not go anywhere."

"I didn't know you cared so much CC."

"I don't. You're the one who has the books. How else are we going to study for this test coming up?"

He mimicked Dave Chappelle's impression of Rick James, *"Cold-blooded."*

Laughter bounced off the crème walls of the small room—a welcomed relief to the tension of studying.

"So, what are ya'll doing tonight?"

"Here we go again. How do you expect to do well in your classes when you're always out doing..." Ciara paused, then rolled her eyes. *"Extracurricular activities?"*

"When I get stressed I can't concentrate. So I need a stress reliever so I can focus on my work."

"You really believe that? Partying *helps* you do well in class?" Faraji asked in a skeptical tone.

"Yeah, it keeps me motivated. Like an incentive."

She wasn't buying it. "And why do you deserve to go out tonight?"

"I wasn't talkin' about party-partying. Was thinking about hanging out on South campus. I know a guy having a get-together at Simpson."

If it was even a fraction of what the Theta party gave him, he would surely forget Eidsvick, Ralph and Renoir after a few sips.

"I'm almost finished with my paper. Might as well celebrate, right?" Faraji said.

"That's as good an excuse as any. What about you CC?"

"Yeah, do you need to text your boyfriend to see if he's okay with you coming out?"

"I don't have to ask his permission," she snapped. "I *choose* not to go out because I have so much work to do."

"Hey, if I were dating a man that fine, I'd want to keep him on lock. You can look at these chicks and tell they're thirsty. Sometimes I want to go up and ask them if they want a drink of water."

"Faraji, you've got a strange way of getting people to do something," Nick said.

"Party's at Simpson Hall, huh?" Ciara muttered. "I guess I could hang out for a little bit."

He and Faraji exchanged looks at how they easily persuaded Miss Innocent to attend a party.

"That's what's up."

If he was going stay or leave—that decision didn't mean he couldn't enjoy the experience to the fullest.

## CHAPTER TEN | *Nick*

They could hear the bass pumping through the door. The dry-erase board of Big Bryce's messages scribbled in black vibrated with each thunder of 808s.

Nick twisted the doorknob. Locked. He pounded on the door.

"Let me text him. 'Cause my knocks are blending in with the music."

"I'm mad they're up in there partying like this," Faraji said, arms crossed.

Was she genuinely mad, cold or having doubts about the low-cut silk top? The gold fabric made her skin glow and he kept reminding himself to look at the curve of her eyebrows instead of her chest.

"Well soon, we'll be up in there partying."

"I don't know about this," Ciara said. No attitude in her voice and no shirt scooping low enough to preview her goods, but her arms were crossed too.

Her eyes scanned slowly from the end of the long, dark hallway. The fluorescent light above the elevator bank buzzed and blinked.

Even in dim lighting, it was easy to tell that Simpson was one of the older dorms.

The navy diamond-patterned carpet and chipping mustard walls had seen their fair share of partying college students. It's only attractive feature were the large suites perfect for said partying.

"We're gonna have fun. Trust me."

"Yeah girl. It's a little gathering. It ain't like..." Faraji's voice drifted as the door suddenly flung open.

Tall and dark in a black t-shirt stretching over his third trimester stomach, Big Bryce almost filled up the entire doorframe. A small white hand towel draped over his shoulder and his chiclet teeth shined antifreeze-green under the black light.

"Faraji and Ciara, this is Big Bryce."

Head nods and 'nice to meet you's were exchanged.

"Ya'll come on in. Punch is over there."

"Ladies first," Nick said.

The speakers banged out Ludacris' simple question: 'How low can you go?' Girls in everything mini competed with each other to prove who could dive to the floor the lowest.

Nick rubbed his hands together, ready to get a red cup in one hand and one of those getting-low girls' hips in the other, when he smashed into Ciara's back.

"Hey, you wanna go on inside? I told you, everything's gonna be straight," he yelled over the thumping music that abruptly transitioned into something slow and seductive.

Still she didn't move.

*This must be her first party ever.*

Disappointed and annoyed that he would have to end his night early and sober, he took a deep breath.

His lips brushed her lobe when he said, "We can leave if you're uncomfortable."

Tears reflecting bright purple, slid down her cheek.

"What's wrong, CC?"

"I guess she didn't ask her boyfriend's permission to go out after all," Faraji said.

Her arms were crossed again—this time accompanying a mean squint. "There he is. Getting it in with some other chick. Thirsty I tell you. I ought to offer the heifer some water."

CHAPTER ELEVEN | *Ciara*

R&B singer Trey Songz passionately gambled that the neighbors knew his name.

The sound of Ciara's heart pounded against her eardrums, a beat as steady as the knocking bass line in the song.

Her mind, body and spirit froze; and she wished she could push CONTROL-ALT-DELETE and END NOW.

"Let's go," Faraji said, linking arms with her.

"Yeah, this party's lame," Nick said. His words were followed with an awkward, pitiful chuckle.

Pity. Everybody shook their heads with pity at the ignorant freshman—she doesn't know any better. Professors, resident advisors and students especially pitied the freshman girl who lost her roommate.

And now as eyes watched her pitifully over the rims of red cups, she was the freshman girl who lost her man.

"No, I'm not going anywhere!"

Trey was singing the hook in Muppet-faced girl's ear and didn't see Ciara coming.

She struck him with small, balled fists dangerously sharp with the very jewels he'd pushed on her finger as a promise of his love.

The party scene turned into a live episode of *Cheaters,* with most of the people so caught off guard by the conflict they stood in the middle of it.

"How could you do this to me? I trusted you!"

Nick wrapped his arms around her waist, but she had the reach of Laila Ali, those red-velvet nails clawing air and flesh.

Trey tried to block the assault against his face with his elbow and talk at the same time. "Listen. Let me explain."

Miss Piggy pushed her and Ciara reached for her long feathered, blond bangs. "Oh, you want to fight me too?"

He pulled Miss Piggy back, the image of Trey holding another woman enraged Ciara more.

The vileness rose so quickly from her belly. Whore, slut and a few other choice phrases spewed from her mouth onto both of them.

She heard the words, felt her hot flesh connecting with theirs and wanted to stop—but the adrenaline pumping through her veins told her to crush them, even if she destroyed herself in the process.

The music switched off.

"Hey, don't make *me* start fighting up in here." Big Bryce's voice was as giant as his build, automatically sobering and silencing them all except Ciara.

Chest heaving up and down, she fought for air. "It's over. Don't call me. Don't stop by. Don't even look at me ever again."

"For real Nick, ya'll need to take your girl somewhere else," Big Bryce said.

"I got it. Come on CC."

He and Faraji towed her away, twisting and forever gazing at the man who was supposed to be hers and hers alone.

## Chapter Twelve | *Nick*

"See why I don't go out?" Ciara said, offering a weak smile.

Nick felt a little guilty for wanting to stay at the party. He didn't see what the big deal was with Trey. The dude looked lame to him. And the girl he was dancing with didn't look any better. She definitely wasn't as pretty as Ciara, so in his opinion, Trey was both lame and stupid.

He and Faraji walked her back to her room and sat with her, joking around and talking about whatever would distract her. They popped a couple bags of popcorn and mocked the student-made shorts on AGU-TV until the station went black.

When she said she was ready for bed, Faraji offered to make it a sleepover. And Nick was down with that too—the night might end up better than he thought!

"I'd rather be alone, but I appreciate ya'll looking out for me."

"Let us know if you need anything, okay girl?" Faraji said, hugging her.

"Wish I would've grabbed one of those cups at Big Bryce's before we got up out of there," Nick said. "This night definitely deserved a drink."

"Do you think she'll be okay by herself?"

"That's how some people cope. Me, I couldn't do it. I'd go crazy staring at the walls."

"I caught my boyfriend like that one time."

Nick stopped in the middle of the hallway. "Wait. What man with any intelligence would cheat on you?"

She showed a row of perfect white teeth and shrugged her shoulders.

"What did you do?"

"What any silly young girl would do? I forgave him. I didn't break up with him until I decided to come here. It's harder when you have to see the person all the time."

"Plus, I mean, coming to AGU you've got options of smarter, better looking men, like myself," he said, stroking his smooth chin.

"You never stop, do you?"

The elevator dinged and Faraji stepped on with him. "Do you mind if I hang out in your room? I'm too worked up to be alone."

"Sure, my roommate's cool."

Even at the late hour, the new-age folksy sounds of Bon Iver spilled out the open door. The melody of murmurings made Faraji frown and mutter: "What in the world?"

Nick was not only used to Kenny's late night jams, but had actually grown to like the music.

"What up Kenny G."

"Chillin'," Kenny said. The beady, black eyes behind Malcolm X-esque brow line glasses were fixed on his laptop screen.

"You still stalking Carmen?" Nick opened his miniature refrigerator stocked with water, fruit punch flavored Gatorade and vodka. He twisted open a bottle and searched for clean glasses.

"I'm not even looking at her profile." His cheeks flushing cotton candy pink, Kenny turned to see their guest sitting on Nick's bed. He nudged his bifocals up the ridge of his hooked nose. "Oh, hey there."

"I'm Faraji."

"Ferrari? Like the sports car?"

"*Fa-rah-GEE*."

"Sorry. I wasn't trying to be racist or anything. I personally like the uniqueness of African American names."

Faraji pointed at Kenny but spoke to Nick. "Is he for real?"

"Nah. He chooses to purposely be an ass sometimes." Nick smiled at the awkward exchange. He glimpsed over Kenny's shoulder at the computer screen. "So what's your girl up to tonight?"

"Like you don't check up on people online. You told me yourself you looked me up when you found out we were roommates."

"Sure did. Thought about asking for somebody else when I saw your busted profile picture."

"I told you, I had a rough senior year. Bad all around."

Nick sat a shot glass filled to the rim onto his *Family Guy* themed mouse pad featuring Stewie. "I didn't expect you to be here tonight."

"Not for long." He clicked the mouse with one hand, waved the other. "You can have at it with your girl."

Faraji narrowed her eyes at Nick across the room. Her lack of a smart, sassy comeback amused him. Kenny G's quips had her speechless.

"It ain't like that. She's just a friend."

"I'm not judging brother," he said, slurping his shot.

Kenny pulled on his backpack, stuffed white buds in his ears. "It was sweet meeting you."

He held out his fist and Faraji obliged him by bumping it.

"What is up with your roommate?" she asked once the door closed.

"Kenny's a little strange sometimes, but for the most part he stays outta my way and I stay outta his."

"He's got those crazy-folks eyes. The way he looked at me. Like he was undressing me."

"You know, he probably likes you."

Faraji slowly crossed her smooth legs. "Everybody likes me. Tell me something I don't know."

"You're alright."

"Baby, I'm the best thing you never had." She lifted the shot glass and finished it in one smooth gulp. "How does the saying go? Grey Goose get you loose? What are you trying to pull?"

"You're the one that wanted to come to my room."

Nick didn't want to, but he stared at her, re-carving each curve of her body. With each twist and turn, the skirt rode further up her thighs. She twirled her brown stiletto sandals playfully, perfect little toes coated in a pink rose color peeked through the straps.

He pushed an image to the back of his mind, brought the shot glass to his lips.

"As my grandma would say, you ain't nothin' but trouble."

\* \* \*

The bright blue light of his cell phone illuminated her face, making the natural confetti on her cheeks pop.

The extra long twin bed was so narrow, they had no choice but to cuddle. He reached across her and she didn't shift.

*It's late and you're probably asleep. But if you're not...I need you.*

The words pulled him from the 'here and now' to that place of 'if.'

Faraji slept so deeply, so peacefully that the only sign that she wasn't dead was the slight lift of her chest. His cheap white cotton sheets wrapped around her body.

She'd drunkenly confessed that she didn't believe in sleeping in clothes during the summertime and he'd drunkenly noted his appreciation for her body.

Then one kiss led to a touch to another and more than he'd imagined.

He wanted to stay and he wanted to go.

He regretted that this might mess up their friendship, but was content in her presence.

Face-to face, he pressed his lips against hers. So soft, the taste of her lingering.

He eased his arm from under her warmness and she rolled away from his embrace into the fetal position.

She moaned a quiet sigh as he eased the door shut, leaving her alone in his bed.

## Chapter Thirteen | *Ciara*

Ciara was surprised at how easy it was to make it to the Caldwell rooftop.

It had only been a little over a month since the incident. After all the investigations and hoopla about security, here she was, perhaps standing in the very place Tala contemplated taking her own life.

Quietness covered the campus. Everyone and life itself slowed down post-midterms.

Every step Ciara took was accented by the crush of gravel beneath her sneakers. There was nothing up there, but empty planter boxes, the hum of machinery and an amazing view.

All of Aurbor Grove—The Village courtyard, Gilbert Dining Hall, the old administrative offices and academic buildings, Bates Student Center, the paper mill—was clear from that vantage point.

Ciara could even see The Clove, a community of project high-rises that sat next-door to AGU's massive acreage.

This had quickly become her new home. Despite everything wrong that had happened, it felt right to be at AGU.

She inched further towards the ledge. The moon was almost full and there were plenty of stars out that shined brighter than the artificial lamps lining campus.

The idea of ignoring the security warnings and climbing to the top of Caldwell Hall came to her after the first time she dreamed about Tala.

It really was a crazy notion. But the dreams kept interrupting her nights and she searched for a way to put an end to them.

Each dream began with the two girls getting along so well, the warm depth of their friendship echoed long after she woke up. However, they all ended differently. The strangest one came to Ciara after she caught Trey at Simpson Hall.

Faraji and Nick had left her in the solitude of her room. Emotionally drained, she fell asleep on the futon quickly.

The dream began like all the others, but swiftly became a nightmare, with a silent Tala wrapping her icy fingers around her neck.

But the scariest part was when Ciara didn't fight her. She invited it.

She breathed the last of the warm night air. It tasted sweet like honey. Serenity fell over her, lulling her to an eternal rest.

Then she woke up, so shaken she was afraid to close her eyes again. Ciara was certain she felt Tala's presence in the room and couldn't take being alone, so she texted Nick.

Maybe she was reacting to Trey's indiscretion in an odd way.

Maybe coming up to the rooftop was just as crazy.

She wanted to believe it would bring some closure or at the very least stop the dreams.

She moved closer to the edge, her heart pounding with a familiar fear. She peeped over, caught a glimpse of Lorena's garden—those red roses, big and open.

*What had it felt like to fall?*

*Was it fast? Did time come to a complete halt?*

*Did Tala get scared?*

Something told her Tala was never afraid of anything. Except living.

It was a fear that she too wanted to overcome.

Chapter Fourteen | *Ciara*


They were late for Professor Garrett's annual student dinner. The exclusive event gave promising freshmen the rare opportunity to meet with AGU's top researchers and professors in a casual, one-on-one setting.

He proudly shared stories with the class, recounting students who met lifelong mentors and dissertation sponsors at his dinners.

This was probably the first time Ciara had been genuinely excited about 'partying' on a Tuesday night.

She was disappointed at their tardiness and the first impression it would make.

Not only was this her chance to develop solid connections and showcase her skills, it was a welcomed distraction from the other side of her life.

She'd climbed to the top of Caldwell eight nights in a row now and each night granted her peaceful, dreamless sleep.

"I didn't know neighborhoods like this existed in Aurbor Grove outside of Greek row. I wonder if Garrett has one of these big houses," Faraji mumbled as Ciara barreled through the streets.

"Professors don't really make that much money."

"I thought they did pretty good. Selling all of their books to us." Faraji flipped the mirror down and reapplied her lipgloss.

"You're really tryin' to get your A tonight, huh?" Nick joked, leaning forward.

Ciara's heart and mind were so clouded with leftover hurt, she almost overlooked the magnitude of silence between her friends. Usually she had to fight to get a word in.

She shot furtive glances at Faraji who ran the shiny peach shade across her bottom lip, back and forth, never responding to Nick.

He stared out the window, square jaw clenching, watching the city whisk by in a blur of gray buildings and muted streetlights.

"Guys, I know what happened at Simpson was...crazy." She cleared away the lump crawling in her throat.

The image of him and *that girl* in his arms was on automatic replay within the theater of her mind.

She forced a smile, gave off an air of confidence. "Just because my love life is a hot mess doesn't mean we have to be awkward around each other. I'm fine."

"What are you talking about, girl?" Faraji popped her lips, wiped away the color outside the lines with her thumb.

"You don't have to lie. I know you probably thought I'd gone off the deep end when I started crying in class today. It's been...hard. I've got to get him out of my system."

Faraji reached over, rubbed the top of Ciara's hand. "I know what you mean," she offered softly.

Their eyes met for a moment and Ciara caught her own pain reflected in the catch lights.

"I thought you were cryin' over your essay grade. I know I wanted to," Nick said.

"You are so silly!"

The navigation system announced that her destination was approaching on the right. She slowed at the two-story colonnade that wrapped around the tall white house.

Half of her expected Scarlett O' Hara to come skipping down the steps her thick black mane bouncing in the wind, drawling, "Ashley."

Tapping her taupe-colored nail against the window, Faraji purred. "Professor Garrett has to have something on the side to live somewhere like this."

She adjusted her dress and ran her hands over the ponytail tickling the nape of her neck.

Faraji was at the front door ringing the doorbell before Ciara could pull her key from the ignition.

"What's going on with her?"

"Maybe it's that time of the month," Nick said.

"You would go there."

"I'm just saying, anytime a woman starts being all bipolar, usually ain't but two reasons: a man or that monthly visit."

"It is never that simple."

"It's always that simple. Ya'll the ones that make it complicated."

He opened the door for her, the chatter and jazz welcoming them into a well-lit foyer. Their shoes echoed against the chocolate and white marble floor.

"There's the remainder of the musketeers." Dr. Garrett's arms were outstretched, small circles of his signature perspiration darkening the underarms of the blue oxford shirt.

"I thought you had skipped out on the main event when Faraji came through alone."

"I wouldn't miss it. You and your wife Natalie have a lovely home. I guess it's not hard to decorate when you have the talent to sculpt masterpieces."

Dr. Garrett tilted his head a little.

*Yeah, I know your wife's name and what she does too.*

She'd thoroughly researched him and the other professors in attendance and couldn't wait to get the same reaction from them all.

That twinkle that lit up their blue/green/brown eyes when they were impressed lifted her self-esteem.

Carolyn drilled in her that Black students had to be five times better than their counterparts; she aimed for ten. Tonight she could use all the lifting she could get.

"Miss Capers, you do not have to kiss up to me. You write like a sophomore and study like a junior."

"Yeah, relax CC. You're making me look bad."

"Ah, buddy, you don't need her for that."

"You sure don't."

"Jokes aside, I'm glad you both could make it."

"I thought it was required?" Nick asked, pointing his finger towards the floor.

"It is, technically. But take advantage of both the free hors d'oeuvres and the conversation."

CHAPTER FIFTEEN | *Nick*

Nick tossed a mini quiche in his mouth, then made his way over to a long table of fruits and vegetables. He wanted another chance at getting Faraji's attention. It was the only reason he'd come to the dinner anyway.

While Ciara was clearly in her element, floating from one professor to the next, he was uncomfortable with the stuffy crowd. He stumbled over his words, his accent eked out. Nobody understood his jokes, the punch lines hanging in silence.

He felt isolated among the other students discussing the impact of climate change, mass incarceration, and Iraq while kissing as much butt as their lips could cover. If this is what it

LAKESHIA POOLE

took to succeed in college, he wasn't sure he wanted it anymore.

"They have some pretty good food up in here," he said.

Faraji ignored him and continued to pick up pieces of honeydew melon and cantaloupe, avoiding his stare. She bit the red tip of an oversized strawberry without realizing how enticing the act was for Nick. He laughed nervously. It looked like she planned to continue the silent treatment. And honestly he deserved it. He never should have left her like that.

"I might need to wrap some up in a napkin and stuff 'em in your purse for lunch tomorrow."

He crossed the table, so close that her sweet scent surrounded him.

She stepped back when Nick reached out, rubbed away a trickle of strawberry juice at the corner of her lip. He remembered her softness and craved it again. Wanted her again.

"Is everything a joke to you?"

"No, I...I want..." he paused because truthfully he wasn't sure what he wanted. "I wanted to make you smile again. I told you I was sorry. I had to leave. It was an emergency."

90

She frowned in disbelief at the sweet words he delivered on top of the pile of excuses.

"What happened...it was a mistake," she said, looking away. "I can't believe I allowed myself to do something like that."

"You act like it was the worst thing ever. I personally enjoyed it. "

"Stop," Faraji whispered.

He eased closer, touched her elbow. "I mean it. I want to see you again. I want us to—"

"I don't want to talk about it. Not here, not now."

"That's fine. I'm just happy that you're talking to me. I can't take the silent treatment, not answering my texts, calls or even talking in class."

She massaged those pearls between her fingertips and looked at him in a way he couldn't decipher.

"What?"

"*Nothing.*"

"You're going to tell me later?"

"Yeah, we can talk later."

He nodded at her handful of fruit. "You on a diet or something?"

Faraji turned up her nose. "I can't do that Freshman 15 thing."

"What are you talking about? You're fine the way you are." He pulled out his vibrating cell phone and groaned.

"I need to answer this. My grandmother will call the campus police if I miss more than two of her phone calls."

He walked a few steps away, speaking low, pacing in a circle.

"What'd she want?"

"She wanted to see if I was coming home for July 4$^{th}$."

"So you're heading back to the country next weekend?"

"Yessir, nobody grills like grandma. While you're busy tryin' to keep away the Freshman 15, I'm losing weight. I ain't had a decent meal since I left."

"I cook a mean Ramen and hotdogs if you ever want to stop by."

Nick made a face. "Naw, that's alright. I'm good on that."

"You too good for Ramen?"

"Everybody don't know how to make Ramen, you know?"

She was leaning in laughing at his favorite bootlegged noodle recipe, when Ciara rushed up.

"We need to go," she said fanning her hands.

"What? Why?" Nick asked.

"I need to go. You can stay if you want to, but I'm leaving. *Right now.*"

*If this dude mess up one more night for me...*

As if reading his mind, Faraji said, "Sweetie, you're gonna have to get over Trey sooner or later."

"It's not Trey!" she cried out, attracting the attention of a few folks nearby before stalking off.

Nick didn't ask any more questions once inside the quiet, leather confines of the car.

He didn't protest when she made rolling stops, sped through red lights and screeched around curves.

But then again he didn't notice the man in the Atlanta Braves hat in the hunter-green Taurus that had been following them since they left The Village parking deck.

CHAPTER SIXTEEN | *Ciara*

Ciara stood fidgeting outside Trey's dorm room, trying not to
appear suspicious to residents walking down the hallway.

She knew his schedule and that his Thursday mornings
were free, so he had to be in there.

She knocked softly. Heard voices behind the door, but
there was no answer.

*Was he alone? Was* she *in there with him?*

*No, I can't do this. I change my mind.*

Before she could bolt down the hallway, the door flung
open.

He didn't hide his shock. "What are you doing here?"

"Can I come in?"

"Yeah, yeah, come on in." She could tell by the immediate spark in Trey's eyes that he thought he had a chance. He looked at her hand—yes his ring was still on her finger.

He paused the movie streaming on his laptop; attempted to straighten up things, tossing clothes and books from the futon to the bed in distinct piles.

"I need to ask you something," she said. "Why don't you sit down next to me?"

He didn't sit close enough to touch her, but she could feel the warmth from his body. She didn't realize how debilitating it could be, being this close to him.

It didn't matter how many times she said she was over him, not hearing his voice or feeling the glide of his fingers across her skin left her numb.

She looked over his shoulder towards the wide window, not wanting him to see what remained there.

"I need your help."

"What's going on?"

"This guy..."

He bristled, brought his fingernails to his mouth.

"It's not like that."

"I didn't say anything. You're single now. You can do what you want," he baited.

She inhaled deeply, then exhaled the pride and hurt that made this conversation so difficult. It drove her crazy that she needed him so bad.

"I didn't come here to rehash the past. We've done plenty of arguing already."

"I'm not arguing," he said, although the timber in his voice spoke a completely different language.

Frustration seeped through: "Will you listen to me?"

"All right, what do you want me to do?"

Ciara grabbed his hand, so large hers fit within it and led him to the window. She leaned in close, his firmness brought back the tingling sensation of security.

She directed his attention to the parking lot. "I need you to help me get rid of him."

Trey frowned, his eyes wandering across the rows of cars. He yelled impatiently, "Who?"

Ciara stabbed the window with her index finger—the print a cross hair for the green Taurus backed under a magnolia tree.

"Him."

Chapter Seventeen | *Nick*

The room was the right temperature–chilly enough to refresh him from the record-high summer heat but not movie theater frigid.

The lights were dimmed, romantically soft. The lilt of Dr. Eidsvick's accent was a sweet lullaby to Nick's eardrums.

"Wake up," Rae said, nudging him before his chin dropped to his chest.

"This class is killin' me." Fridays were the worst because all he could think about was the impending weekend.

Rae wrote down Dr. Eidsvick's words so quickly that he could hear the pen scribbling against the desk.

"Your midday naps are *killing* your GPA. He's already covered like two chapters since you fell asleep."

97

He glanced down at his notes: The Roman numeral one, the word BAROQUE and a trail of illegible letters.

In the right corner, he drew the face of the girl with blond dreads a row down. He touched up her nose and added bamboo beads around her neck.

*I think her name's Phoebe.*

It was easy to forget her name, hard to forget her pimpled face and those white dreads tangled together in a messy, half-ponytail. She passed out flyers to hip-hop events every Monday, Wednesday and Friday after class.

"I can't believe you're over there sketching like this is a high school art class or something."

Nick had impressed Rae with his rendition of her within his margins only a few days ago. Her beauty intimidated him. How could he capture it with a cheap pen?

He'd obsessed over perfecting those olive-green eyes that were set a part a little. The flow of auburn locks and the way the shadows curved out the profile of her face.

"It's nice though, ain't it?"

"No. And you better not ask me for my notes."

For the remainder of the two-hour lecture, he jotted down a few notes, but deep down he didn't see the point in trying.

Nick's grade in Art History held steady at a high C and he was sure he could bring it up with the final exam to a decent B.

He promised himself—his academic advisor, his God and Lucille—that he would take Fall semester seriously.

He needed to break college in, like a pair of stiff-leather loafers. Maybe the more he wore this life, day-by-day, the more confident and comfortable he'd feel waking up and putting it on.

"I know you said I couldn't see them, but I just need to fill in a few blanks. I promise I won't ask for your notes no more."

"I don't think so," Rae said with a smile, pulling on her backpack.

After class, Phoebe stood outside with a stack of red, green and black glossy handbills.

"Hey, I wanted to invite you to the artist showcase going down at Graffiti tonight."

Nick took one, but didn't bother to look at it before tossing it in the trash.

"I might have some notes for you," Rae said. "But only if you go with me to Phoebe's thing downtown."

Nick opened his mouth to object.

*If someone saw me there with her…*

"Don't try to come up with a lie and say you are studying tonight. We both know better."

## CHAPTER EIGHTEEN | *Nick*

*Snooze.*

Nick kept hitting the button on his alarm for the next hour.

"Your girl's downstairs."

Kenny slammed the door hard enough to jerk him awake. He kicked off his tan Rainbow flip-flops, pinching his green Ninja Turtles t-shirt away from the flab of his chest.

"I can't believe it's this hot so early in the morning."

Nick dug in his eye sockets with the heel of his palms, rubbing away sleep and applying pressure to the pounding headache.

Big Bryce had challenged him to a Bacardi 151 contest at Graffiti. Nick lost the competition, but somehow convinced Rae to participate in a nude portrait at her place.

"Where'd you see her? Outside? Front desk?" Nick questioned, tossing toiletries in a plastic Target bag.

"Talking with Scarlett at the front desk. And she looked pretty pissed. Does said pissivity have anything to do with you stumbling in here three hours ago?"

"Your voice...has a way of making a hangover feel ten times worse, you know that?"

"You want me to go get her?"

"Nah, I'm good. I already got my stuff together."

Nick moved fast, knocking over a few bottles and books in the process.

He pulled an ice-cold water from the fridge and splashed his face. He sprayed some cologne under his arms then pulled a Polo on over his white t-shirt.

"Vodka and cologne. That's always a good combination."

"It's gonna have to do. You said she was pissed, so I know I don't have time to take a shower," he said, rolling his luggage out.

"Alright, brother."

Before Kenny could return to scrolling through the messages Carmen posted, Nick poked his head through the door.

"If anybody stops by, tell them I went home. You ain't gotta go into detail."

"You know I wouldn't do that."

"And stop stalking Carmen."

Kenny ignored the last command, bidding Nick goodbye with a fat middle finger.

Scarlett was slowly explaining visitor rules when he walked through the glass door separating residents from visitors.

"Babe, why didn't you let me know you were here?"

She held up a glittery, hot pink encapsulated phone. "I called you at least a dozen times. *At least.*"

"I'm sorry. You know I don't get a good reception behind these prison walls."

He acknowledged Scarlett and thanked her for helping out his girl, because he knew DAs were the gatekeepers and could cause problems later.

"Whatever, let's go. I'm hungry."

"Can you help a brother out?" She grabbed the Target bag.

Nick dragged his laundry bags down the ramp leading to the Roskill turnaround. She aimed the remote and the sleek BMW chirped and the trunk popped open simultaneously.

She watched him do the heavy lifting, hands on her narrow hips. "What are you doing, moving back home for good?"

"Lucille's gonna wash up a few loads for me."

"Oh, so now she's Lucille? We're a little full of ourselves after a couple months of college, huh?"

She pushed on a pair of ivory Gucci sunglasses that matched her short romper.

He found his matching shades in her glove compartment. Reached over and clasped her hand resting on the gear, offered her a simple kiss on the lips.

"I really appreciate you coming to pick me up, babe."

"I have to be certified to wake up at 4 a.m. on a Saturday morning to pick up your funky butt."

"Well Jasmine, ain't that what girlfriends are for?"

"You're right. I've missed you so much. I might not bring you back."

## Chapter Nineteen | *Nick*

Nick had lived with Lucille long enough to forget the face of his real mother.

As soon as he turned 18 he'd memorialized her on his arm.

His six-year old mind had taken a mental Polaroid of the night Lucille learned she'd lost her youngest, breaking down into his Uncle Keith's arms under the porch-light.

Cynthia died in a car accident that involved drugs somehow—but those were the only details he knew.

Lucille always gave him the vague answer that she 'fell in with the wrong crowd' which led to a stern warning and her no list: no liquor, no drugs and no lying.

She said she saw the spirit of his mother within him, but she aimed to tame it with a busy school and church schedule. He didn't have time to consider falling into the wrong crowd.

It appeared to have worked. Lucille raised the first future college graduate from the Barclay name.

Fists on her wide hips, she stood on the concrete porch waiting for him, when Jasmine pulled into the driveway.

The Barclay home sat on a few acres of land and everyone in the neighborhood was related somehow.

Lucille had planted a row of plum bushes and peach trees near the gas tank. When she hit her late 60s she stopped growing vegetables in her gardens.

Nick didn't realize how much he missed it all until he saw her—those deep-set gray eyes and the single black braid that fell to the center of her back.

He was a little self-conscious about last night's smell attached to his clothes, but she didn't say anything about it.

"My baby. It feels like it's been more'n a couple months," she said, holding him in her arms for a while.

She stepped back to inspect him from head to toe. "Looks like you need to eat something."

"Yes, I'm ready. Is the food ready?"

"Soon, soon. I need you to go pick up a few things before everybody gets here."

Jasmine struggled to pull one of his bags behind her. "Hi, Miss Lucille."

"Hey child." Lucille offered her a cheek. "How is the pastor doing?"

"Daddy's fine. He said he'd come over later on."

"Help her with that bag, Nick." She linked arms with Jasmine and they went into the house.

Lucille loved the fact that he dated the preacher's daughter and treated Jasmine like one of her own.

He should have been happy that his grandmother liked his girlfriend, given her high standards, but their attachment worried him.

* * *

After showering, he spent most of the day running errands— getting ice, this specific kind of flour, and a particular cut of pork-chops.

He almost forgot how small the town was, running into cousins and former classmates at each location.

The stop at Walmart nearly turned into a mini class reunion, between the frozen food aisles.

They all asked how he was doing, remarked how different he looked and sounded only after a few months.

Jasmine chauffeured him around, complaining about how they wouldn't get a chance to spend any quality time together.

"I didn't know I was going to have to do all this stuff, okay?"

Less than twenty-four hours of Sandersville, Lucille, Jasmine and everything else that came with being home had him fiending for his life four hours away.

"Do you miss it?"

"Huh?" he said, taken by her mind-reading skills.

"Do you miss Sandersville?"

"Oh." He paused as if deeply considering his final answer. "Hell no."

She gripped the steering wheel tighter, glancing back and forth from the gray highway to him.

"Why do you have to say it like that?"

"I'm happy to be away, that's all. I didn't do anything but catch hell here."

"Oh, hell doesn't exist in Aurbor Grove, huh?"

Nick sighed, the taste of his foot in his mouth bitter.

It wouldn't be long before the tears came. Jasmine could deliver the waterworks better than White Water, then blame it on her Cancer nature.

"That didn't come out right."

"This is our home. My home! You meant it like you said it."

"No, I—"

"I knew you were going to change. I didn't think it'd be this soon," she said decisively.

"Hey, relax, before you swerve off the road."

She purposely zigzagged down the yellow dashes, tires thumping against the center reflectors.

"Watch out, Jasmine!"

"We haven't been in Sandersville a full day, and you're already working my nerves," she muttered, speeding past a kaolin truck filled with a mound of the pure, white mineral.

"Why can't we be happy together?"

"Slow down," he shouted. "You're acting crazy."

"Well, maybe I'm just out of my mind." Plumes of red dust enveloped the car as she pulled off the road abruptly onto a dead-end dirt road.

"What are you doing?"

"That's a good question."

She crossed her arms, twisted in the seat so that she faced Nick straight on.

"What are you doing down there?"

"At AGU?"

"Yeah at AGU. Where else would I be talking about? Stop stalling."

"Going to class. Hanging out with my roommate, classmates. Taking tests."

"You make it sound so boring. And yet you hate Sandersville so much?"

"It's not boring. It's different. You wouldn't understand it."

"Oh, 'cause I'm not at some big deal university like you?"

"Stop putting words in my mouth trying to start an argument."

"Who are you messing with down there?"

"Stop playing games. Let's go, man."

"I wanna know!"

"What makes you think I would do anything like that?"

"Because I know you. And if I hadn't said that you could do it, you would've done it anyway."

He'd convinced himself that it wasn't cheating. That it was just sex. And he did have Jasmine's permission after all. Somewhere within the blurry, gray area of their relationship, things had changed.

"Who is she?"

Nick sighed, Faraji's face flashing in his mind. Those sweet, soft lips brushed across his cheek; her body twisted in his sheets; her scent filled his nostrils.

"Why did you tell me to do it?"

Jasmine's face contorted, displaying her mental anguish. "I don't know. I wasn't ready. It's what you wanted, right? Your freedom to do what you always wanted."

"I did, but...this. What we're doing, it ain't right."

"I figured if you got some of that out of your system, I'd be ready eventually. But all I can think about is if she's prettier than me. Smarter than me. I mean, I know she's one thing better than me," she said.

"That doesn't make anyone better than you. I've always respected your decision to save yourself for marriage."

"It's hard to respect that hundreds of miles away."

She leaned across the console, cupping his face in her hands. Brought his lips to hers and gave him everything–the saltiness of her tears mixed with all of the confusion, happiness, sadness, excitement, love and hate within her heart.

He kissed her back, just as deeply, searching. But he didn't feel anything and she missed the disappointed look on his face.

"I booked us a hotel room," she said, softly. "If you want to, I will."

CHAPTER TWENTY | *Nick*


Jasmine's offer weighed on his mind the rest of the ride home. He tried to downplay the excitement of finally getting to the level he'd always wanted; ignored the rumblings of doubt and consequences of what came with that level after the pleasure.

"You okay?" she asked.

"I'm great, beautiful. Are you sure?"

Unbuckling her seatbelt, she smiled at him, speaking confidently, "I want you because I love you."

"Me too."

The remainder of the family crowded the front yard. Nick's young cousins ran around shooting water guns at each other.

He told them not to let Lucille see their playful warfare as she didn't believe in kids playing with guns of any kind.

A steady stream of smoke from the grill floated from the backyard, making his stomach rumble with hunger.

"I'll go help Miss Lucille get the food together," Jasmine said, carrying their groceries inside.

"Who's this cool cat right here?" a man asked behind him.

*Uncle Keith.*

As Nick walked towards him sitting on the bed of his red F-150, he showed off big, yellow-stained teeth. Keith only came around every once in a while, but Nick felt closer to him than most of his relatives.

He had been to jail for petty stuff and hadn't stepped inside a church since Cynthia died.

"Mama cooking up a storm, like you a VIP or something?"

"Hey I learned from the best."

"How's it going? I heard Mama put you on the prayer list at church the past two weeks," he snickered, pointing the cigarette between his fingers.

"I don't know why. I'm straight."

"Cynthia would be proud," he said. "I know I am. Ain't no jobs here. *Nothing* to do. I hope you livin' it up at AGU."

"I wouldn't say that. But you only get to go to college once."

"I still don't see how you decided to go to that redneck school."

Although they said they were happy and proud of him, there always was a caveat. Family, friends and teachers expressed reasons for him not to attend AGU when he applied, got accepted, went to orientation and now after enrollment.

It's too far away. Cost too much money. Not enough black people. Wasn't Christian enough. It's a party school.

Those were all the reasons he decided to attend the university.

He didn't want to stay close enough for Lucille to pop up unannounced or live content in a world where all the students were a shade of brown. And he loved to party. It was a win-win-win situation.

Nick lifted his chin. "What you got in that cup, old man?"

"Grown folks drink." He held his palm over the plastic cup and eyed Nick suspiciously. "How old are you?"

"Eighteen."

"You started drinkin' yet?"

Nick shrugged the question off. "I might have had a little something."

Keith poured him a half-full cup of his brown-colored concoction.

"Don't let Mama see you drink it neither. No liquor. No drugs. No lying."

He took a sip, its cheap, strong flavor made him cough. "I see you had the rules too."

"We all did. Me and your mama though...we were always outside of 'em."

"For real?"

"Yessir. Always in trouble. Mama said me and Cynthia had the same rebellious spirit. She gave us extra discipline."

"Well, that's how grandma is.

Nick gulped down the rest of his drink, more so because it tasted nasty.

Keith chuckled at his quick finish. "You definitely got that from your mama. Here have another lil' taste."

## CHAPTER TWENTY ONE | *Nick*

"I wanna thank You Lord for our laying down last night.
Thank You for our early rising this mornin'. It was You Lord
that clothed me in my right mind..."

Deacon Collier fervently delivered prayer, supplication
and thanksgiving. His words came out raspy and heavy, rising
up and down in a singsong. Tambourine rolls, shouts of
Amen and Hallelujah from the pulpit and congregation
encouraged him.

"You're a healer."

*"Yeah!"*

"A heart fixer."

*"Thank ya Lord!"*

"*Mind* regulator!"

Hands clasped between his legs, Nick opened one eye to look at his black, square-faced watch. Church service was winding down after two and a half hours.

"I need to go to the bathroom," he whispered in Jasmine's direction.

"You can't get up and leave before benediction."

"Brother needs to hurry it up. It's the offering basket."

"He's almost finished," Jasmine assured. She then repeated along with Deacon Collier's closing, "And when I've done all that I could do. I pray to one day hear you say, 'Well done, my good and faithful servant. Well done.' Amen."

"I swear he's been praying that same prayer for the last 10 years," Nick said, rising.

He felt Lucille's eyes on him as Deacon Collier—led by the spirit he announced—began an impromptu Baptist hymn full of 'O's, 'thee's and 'thou's.

Exiting before the appropriate time was a simple infraction, but a symbol of disrespect duly noted by Lucille and the usher dressed in a crisp white suit.

By the time he finished, service had officially concluded and the sanctuary clamored with music and everyone greeting each other.

Nick watched Lucille fellowship, talking excitedly to the choir director, worn bible in the crook of her arm.

It would take her a while to make her rounds, culminating with a handshake and an invitation to dinner that Pastor Stephens almost always respectfully declined.

He couldn't face them. He didn't want to answer their questions or knowing looks. Or lie and say everything was alright.

No liquor. No drugs. No lying. One out of three wasn't entirely bad, but he headed to the car anyway.

"Not so fast," Jasmine called out. "Miss Lucille's looking for you. She wants Daddy to pray over you."

"It's gonna be six o' clock before we get out of here. Can we pretend that we left already?"

"No. After she saw you with that drink yesterday, we have to exorcise this demon!" she laughed.

"That's not even funny. Uncle Keith set me up. I ended up promising her that I would never drink again."

"Are you going to keep it?"

He shoved his hands in his pockets. "I don't know. She started talking crazy about how we have the gene."

"Gene for what?"

He exhaled, finally replying, "Alcoholism. Things got pretty bad between us. I think when she saw me and how I was acting, it made her think about Cynthia and losing her."

"That's understandable. It's not like you *need* it, right?" Her eyebrows rose when he didn't answer immediately.

"No. I don't see nothin' wrong with having a little drink every now and then."

"Oh, shoot here she comes." Pastor Stephens trailed Lucille who smiled, but it wasn't the friendly kind. That long braid, whipped back and forth with each step down the aisle.

"Uh-oh. Do you think they know about us?" he joked, but felt bad at the immediate embarrassment that came over her face.

"Why would you say that?" she shrieked, all of the color draining from her face. "Oh my goodness. Daddy's gonna kick me out the house."

"Baby, I'm playing. They don't know." He rubbed her back, then leaned down to whisper in her ear: "It's our little secret."

\* \* \*

The car remained silent for most of the ride back to Aurbor Grove.

Nick hated leaving Lucille—especially now that she thought he might have a drug problem—but he was so ready to arrive at *his* home.

He found himself getting excited as they approached the city limits. The paper mill jutted out of the sky—a tie-dye of blue, purple and white. He was even okay with its funky smell permeating the air.

"I can't go back to being without you. Not like this," Jasmine blurted out. It was as if she finished a thought that had been churning for a while.

"I'll be home before you know it," he said, scratching the back of his neck.

"That's not good enough," she sniffled.

"Babe, I don't want you to take this the wrong way, but..."

"But what? Here you go bursting my bubble."

"Don't assume what I'm gonna to say is wrong."

"I'm not. You're so negative sometimes."

"You can't stay here," he spat out. She missed the defiance in his voice, only concerned with their perfect life together in her bubble.

"I could live here. Well maybe not here in your dorm room. We could get an apartment together."

Nick ran his fingers through her silky locks. So beautiful. So innocent. Once. He'd tainted her and hated himself for it.

If only he could rewind the past few days and get a do-over.

He should say something. No, she was too fragile to handle that kind of truth right now.

"I don't know I feel like this whole weekend was a sign. We're meant to be together."

She smiled, her eyes on the road ahead and their future together.

CHAPTER TWENTY TWO | *Ciara*


The noise of a raucous group of know-it-alls fussing over Madden poured out of Faraji's open door into the hallway.

Ciara knocked, but didn't step inside.

"Hey, what's up?" Faraji asked, mid-laugh, rising from the futon.

"I was bored. Thought I'd stop by and see what you were up to tonight?"

"Just hanging out with some friends."

She went from Faraji's smoky eyelids to her wavy mane and the black top embroidered with the word FIERCE hanging off her shoulder. Black 4-inch heels made her bronzed legs look like strong and shapely 400m-runner legs.

"You're all dressed up."

"Big Bryce is having a party downtown later. We're doing a little pre-gaming."

The guys in the background grew louder with accusations of cheating and she closed the door on them.

"What's going on with you, CC? Ever since we went to Garrett's, you've been acting weird. Did I do something to you?"

"I've been stressed out over classes and...you know who."

"You're still thinking about that loser? You need to let go!"

"It's not that easy. I can't just *let go*. Maybe you don't know that because you haven't loved like I love."

"I know it's hard. Before I got here, my ex was the most controlling guy you could imagine."

When Ciara didn't say anything, she carried on. "I wasn't happy, but he made me feel like I had to stay. What I'm saying is, it doesn't seem like you *want* to get over him."

"Little things make me think about him," she said. "And it's not like I have a long line of guys waiting to be with me."

Faraji moved closer and Ciara expected her to extend a hug.

"Nick told me that it was you he came to see that night."

Her first instinct was to play things off. But Faraji could sense a lie like a bloodhound tracking down hemoglobin.

"I-I needed someone. After I told you guys I was fine, I realized how much I wasn't." She stopped short of sharing how Tala visited her in a dream. And how remnants of her spirit seemed to linger in the room. Ciara had never believed in ghosts, but she couldn't deny that Tala's death changed her.

"Did anything happen between the two of you?" Faraji asked.

"What? Are you crazy?"

"You don't have to get all defensive. I thought it was strange you didn't mention it to me," Faraji said. "Or ask me."

"I didn't know I needed your permission to invite Nick over?"

"No, I'm asking...why didn't you want me to come see you?"

Ciara pursed her lips, unsure of the best response.

"I thought we were closer. I don't know too many chicks here. I figured I could count on you and you could count on me."

Faraji was like Carolyn–the need to be needed ran deep.

"Wait, hold up. You think we're not cool anymore because I reached out to Nick instead of you?"

"What am I supposed to think?"

"That I didn't call you because I wasn't trying to slash any tires or throw bricks through his window." Ciara broke into laughter, listing the many ideas of revenge Faraji offered that night.

Seconds later Faraji laughed right along with her.

"I needed some peace, not to start a war."

"I may have overreacted a teensy, weensy bit."

"If I called you, we would've been kicked out of AGU. I know you've got my back."

"Good. I'm sorry I get excited and can go overboard sometimes."

"Which is why I'm glad you've got *my* back."

"So now that we've gotten that Hallmark moment out of the way. You hanging tonight?"

"Oh, so I'm invited to hang out with you again?"

Faraji rolled her eyes. "I *was* acting a lil' stank earlier. I'm woman enough to admit that."

"A little morning-breath funky."

Faraji reached for the doorknob. "Well come on in, so I can introduce you to my friends. I'm positive they'll make you forget all about Trey."

Ciara stopped, holding up her finger.

"I'll go out with you guys on one condition."

"What's that?"

"You need to tell me what *you* were doing with Nick the night I called him."

"See, what had happened was..."

CHAPTER TWENTY THREE | *Ciara*

Inferno's mirrored walls reflected red lights meant to invoke thoughts of hell. With all the people packed in the narrow space, it felt like hell too.

The club was a popular spot for good music and cheap drinks for both students and locals, oftentimes making it a breeding ground for fights between the two groups.

The DJ with blue-spiked hair and piercings all over, spun top hip-hop hits and pushed out billows of cold air from his smoke machine.

"Hey girl, get up here!"

Faraji moved like a professional go-go dancer atop the U-shaped bar. Tangerine clutch in hand, not a hair out of place, she swayed to the Beyonce blaring throughout the club. Even the bright 21+ wristbands Big Bryce gave them matched her ensemble.

After a few drinks, she didn't stumble, exhibiting perfect balance in stilettos, unlike some of the other bar counter dancers that gyrated off-tempo.

Ciara sat comfortably in a round black booth across from the bar, watching the show.

*Maybe that's why all of the guys like her.*

She was the picture of the "perfect" guy's girl. She talked football and obsessed over Halo as much as she did hair, nails and fashion.

"So how long have you known Faraji?" one of the guys barked in her ear.

"I met her this summer."

Ciara wished she could remember his name. She only recalled that he was from South Georgia and was a starter for the upcoming football season, which explained all the jealous looks she garnered from other girls.

*Ricky. Patrick. Tim?*

She was afraid she might call him the wrong name and lose his interest. She wanted him to stay there. At 6'4" he towered over her, his presence and charm a magnet.

He was like Beyonce's personal bodyguard. In fact his build and pointed baldhead resembled the guy.

"How did you two meet?" she asked, but didn't bother to really listen to his long story.

Ciara came out—not for the free drinks, music or to meet her next boyfriend—only to lay a trap.

She felt guilty about showing up at Faraji's room with ill intentions, but Trey said his plan would work better with witnesses. He told her he would put an end to it all.

They were supposed to meet at midnight. She checked the time display on her phone for the hundredth time. It remained 12:45 a.m. and still no Trey.

Atlanta Braves Hat followed her downtown to Inferno, as she knew he would. She didn't expect for him to try anything too crazy in a public place.

Her stalker sat at the far end of the bar pretending to be engrossed in the sport replays airing on the big-screen TV hanging over the shelves of liquor. No one paid attention to him, even though his age should have made him stand out among the young crowd. Everyone was too busy getting the last bit of party out of their systems before finals.

It took every ounce of her being—and a shot of liquid courage—to stay calm and convince herself that despite Trey's absence it would all work out.

"Hey, do I sense a love connection over here?" Faraji's voice startled her from her thoughts; the phone tumbled from her hands onto the grimy floor.

"Here you go," she started, then snatched the phone back. "This is what I'm talking about."

She shoved the phone in Ciara's face.

*Trey: will b there n a fw*

"Why do you still have his number saved in your phone?"

"It's not like that. He's helping me."

"No. No. No. He is toxic. This calls for an intervention," Faraji slurred, scrolling through the phone. With a few taps on the screen, she deleted the message and his contact information.

It didn't matter. Trey's number was inscribed in her heart. But to keep from attracting unnecessary attention she let Faraji complete her dramatic monologue.

"Let go! And if he shows up I'm gonna get Tyler, Cam *and* Big Bryce on him."

She glanced over her bare shoulders, shimmering with gold. Atlanta Braves Hat sipped on his fifth Miller High Life, eyes glued to the flat screen.

"Are you even listening to me?"

"Yes, do you think it would be okay if I go to the bathroom?"

"Real funny," Faraji huffed, then a forgiving beat later. "You want me to come along?"

"I think I can handle the toilet by myself. Besides I need you to save my seat. These heels are killing my feet."

"I don't think so." Faraji plucked the phone from her hands. "No toilet texting Trey."

Ciara slid through the crowd, her mind working.

*What if Trey thinks it's off?*

*I need to get my phone back.*

*What if he shows up and Faraji sees him?*

*How am I going to link up with him without causing a scene?*

The questions kept coming as she hovered over the toilet.

The one-stall bathroom was fairly clean, bearing only a few scribbles about who slept with who, a handful of phone numbers and some other crazy inscriptions.

She splashed a handful of cold water across her face and dried it with a rough, brown paper towel.

"Get it together. This ends tonight." She tried to pump herself up, but the reflection staring back at her was dead-scared.

*What does he want from me?*

She reapplied her lip-gloss, smoothed her hands down the black, jersey dress and tried to shake off fear.

She wished she would've asked Beyonce's bodyguard to accompany her to the bathroom, but he probably would have gotten the wrong idea.

Her smile disappeared and her heart sank into her stomach. She gasped, the odor of beer and cigarettes on his breath.

"Miss Capers."

## Chapter Twenty Four | *Ciara*

Ciara reminded herself to breathe. Her legs wobbled in the gold sandals.

She tried to conceal the fear pumping through her veins running so fast she could feel the vibration in her fingertips. But her rosy cheeks and sweaty forehead put fear on display.

Somehow she formed a sensible question, "Wh-what do you want from me?"

"Why do you think I'm here?" His accented voice was doubly threatening and soothing. He was from the South, but sounded more Texas than Georgia.

For a businessman he dressed casually—navy t-shirt, Wranglers and Reeboks. And of course his signature Atlanta Braves hat.

He didn't even try to blend in to the background. It didn't matter because Ciara never forgot him after the first time they met.

Though Mr. Bing mentioned his new hired help, the man caught her off guard showing up at her door the next day, asking ridiculous questions. He intended to find her culpable for Tala's death and claimed to have evidence contrary to the police's suicide ruling. He said he was an ex-cop and that everybody knew that politics had gotten in the way of police work.

When she refused to talk anymore, he kept showing up. Outside the auditorium. In the dining hall. At freshman seminar outings. In The Village, a posted stamp of guilt.

It was like he wanted to push her to the edge.

She ignored his phone calls, but he continued to leave the same message about finding out the truth. He bragged about how much money Mr. Bing was giving him and that he wasn't going to let up until he earned every red cent of his payment.

After a while she began to wonder if she was imagining that tattered navy hat with the cursive white 'A.'

*Was it possible for him to be so omnipresent?*

"I left messages. I stopped by. You can't seem to ever 'member to return my call. Makes me wonder if you were lyin' to me?"

"Get away from me!" The music was too loud for anyone to notice her cry for help. Her vocal chords were no match for T-Pain's auto-tune chorus blasting overhead.

"What're you doing?" he smirked.

He moved in closer, forcing her to back further into the secluded hallway filled with the scent of alcohol, urine, sweat and her fear. She bumped against the antique jukebox used more for décor than its musical selections.

"I want to talk you. Not scare you."

"I told you everything I know. All that I could remember from what happened that night."

He crossed his bulky arms, the veins thick and winding under his peach-toned skin. He switched the toothpick dangling from his lips from the left side to the right with his tongue.

"Why do you keep avoidin' me if you got nothin' to hide?"

"I didn't do anything wrong. And I don't want you twisting my words so you can have a case."

"You don't feel like you contributed...*at any point* to the death of Tala Bing?"

"I didn't know she wanted to kill herself. I didn't know her."

"So you believe that she committed suicide?"

"That's what happened."

"Don't you think it's a little suspicious that someone with a life like Miss Bing would jump off of a building? I mean she had a daggone full ride. Rode around in a nice car. Didn't want for a darn thang. Daddy took care of everything."

"Like I've said before, I didn't know her that well."

"How did you come to live together?"

She hunched her shoulders, voice full of attitude, "Random selection like thousands of other freshmen?"

"Did you notice if she was a lil' down a few days before her death?"

"You've read the police report. I don't understand why you keep harassing me. And following me."

She didn't think he could get closer, but he did. His belly protruded, pushing against his shirt.

"You're gonna lead me to the truth. I can *feel it.*"

"I'm going to call the police."

He laughed, head tossed back, revealing a few silver-filled cavities.

"And tell 'em what?"

"I'm going to get a restraining order."

He rubbed his stout fingers together, feeling onto something invisible. "You can tell me. Did you kill her?"

"CC, what's going on!?" One hundred and thirty pounds of fierceness came barreling through the crowd.

Atlanta Braves Hat removed his toothpick, turning around to see the 5'8" threat in stilettos.

"She's cute," he said, winking. "See you later CC. I promise if you wave at me in the rearview, I'll wave back, okay?"

She watched his fat legs move slowly against each other, brushing past Faraji.

Faraji stopped in the middle of a group of people, to stare him down. "Who the hell was that?"

Ciara scratched the arch of her brow. "Some random guy."

"If he's so random, why was he all up on you like that?"

"What are you talking about?"

"Don't tell me you're trying *something new*, girl," Faraji looked back for the guy. "I know Trey was a mess, but you don't have to go there."

"He was some drunk old guy trying to hit on me. That's all."

"Speaking of which, Tyler has been asking about you all night."

"Look at you, Miss Love Connection."

"I try to make it happen. I saw the way the two of you were looking at each other back at the Village."

"Whatever."

"Come with us to Waffle House. He said he wanted to talk to you outside of this loud club."

"I don't know about that."

Atlanta Braves Hat's face appeared in her mind and his words resounded in her ears.

She didn't want to be alone. She needed her bodyguards. Both Sasha Fierce Faraji and Beyonce bodyguard Tyler.

"I'll come."

CHAPTER TWENTY FIVE | *Ciara*

"You don't think the terrorists had anything to do with that oil spill?" Aaron asked.

Tony half-smiled. "You are always coming up with these ridiculous theories. And you have no proof."

"You want them to have a press conference or something?"

They were the only group of people crowded around a table in the student center lounge. Flat screen TVs overhead showcased the latest news and a soap opera. The area with its cedar highboy tables, living room-worthy furniture and snack stand was meant for breaks between classes.

Aaron had staged a coup to make it his own debate hall, with Tony, Ciara and Faraji serving as his audience.

"They buried the truth. Look it up. And don't get me started on Katrina."

"No, we don't want to *get you started*," Ciara said. "But you have to admit, you are always coming up with the most radical reason for things."

"When are Black people going to pull their heads out of the sand and take a stand for something?"

"Here we go," Tony muttered. He shoved books in his backpack and pulled the straps onto his broad shoulders.

Ciara stifled a laugh, catching Faraji's open-mouth gaze. She couldn't hide admiration if her life depended on it.

"I'll let you both have him to yourself."

"See you later Tony." Faraji smiled and watched him all the way to the sliding doors.

"I see you fell for the light skin, light eyes," Aaron said, shaking his head.

He patted his chest, then caressed his own cheeks and goateed chin. "All this smooth, dark chocolate over here and you ogling Pretty Tony."

"Aaron, you know you're my favorite," she began, reaching over and sliding her finger down his arm. "But you don't ever go to class! You're a bad influence."

Ciara laughed, because it was true. Aaron was always at the student center and usually in this same spot holding court. Some days she wondered if he was even a registered, AGU student.

"Check it out," he said, waving towards the sliding door entrance.

An orientation counselor with long legs and wavy brunette tresses led a small group of bright-eyed teens. "Freshman orientation. How many Black folks you see? One, two, uh-oh, three. That's a record."

"Why are you being so pessimistic? We're Black. We're here," Ciara said.

"AGU is not doing all it can and should be doing to attract a more diverse student body."

"Yes, they could do much more, but so could we. Why don't we organize programs that attract more minorities to look at AGU?"

"No, let me tell you something." He raised a finger, then dropped it to the table with a thud. "It starts from the top down. And we all know that Gilmore thinks black boys are only good for one thing: playing football. He could give a damn if they actually graduate."

"Time out. How are we going to solve the world's problems sitting around Bates?" Faraji asked. "And never going to class?"

"Look, I'm puttin' ya'll freshman onto the real. If you can't handle it, that's on you."

"I love to argue, but I swear you make my head hurt. Even when you're right," Ciara groaned.

"CC you ready to head out? Garrett said if I'm late one more time, he's dropping me a letter grade."

"Alright go on ahead. We'll finish this conversation later," Aaron said.

"See you later."

"Here in the same place, I'm sure," Faraji laughed.

"You wanna walk or take the shuttle?"

"Can't risk the shuttle being late. I need the workout, anyway."

"You are all of 100 pounds," Ciara said.

"I wish. That dining hall food is no good. Patty melt. Pizza. Cheeseburger. Pasta. French-fries."

"It does get old after a while."

"And fattening. I have to keep it right and tight for my boo."

"Who? Tony?"

"Girl, please. He's pretty to look at, but he's got too much going on." She paused, to take a deep breath, striding slowly up Ashford. "A man that fine always comes with baggage. Especially when he's a sophomore."

"You never know."

"No, but I do believe that Tyler is a nice guy. He's not your stereotypical football player."

"If you want to know something, come straight out and ask it."

"So what did ya'll do after Waffle House?"

"Nothing. He walked me to my room."

Faraji stopped both for the dramatic effect and to catch her breath.

"Well *I heard...*"

Those words made Ciara stop, bite the corner of her mouth like a toddler expecting a spanking.

"He kissed me first. It was nice. We spent the night together. He didn't trying anything."

"Girl, who knew you had it in you?"

"It wasn't a big deal. We called it a night. He left. We've texted a couple times, but I haven't seen him since then."

"Aw, I love making love connections," Faraji said. "I thought you were going to kill me for not letting you get your phone and talk to Trey."

"I almost did."

"Us women are always fighting over men. Both the ones we love and the ones we hate. I was trying to protect you."

"That night...you don't understand. He loves me, despite whatever he did. She might've had him for that one night, but I'll always have his heart."

"That's crazy talk."

"That's love."

"Well, crazy, does he still have yours?"

Ciara didn't answer. She didn't have to.

CHAPTER TWENTY SIX | *Nick*

When his grade plummeted to the D-F range, Nick decided to forget pride and looking stupid and pay Eidsvick a visit.

He held onto the doorknob, practicing the best manner of begging for a second chance.

"Are you going to try to pass my class?" Dr. Eidsvick asked, before he could even lay out his case.

No good morning, how are you, the man got straight to the point—something that he struggled with during his lectures.

It surprised and slightly embarrassed Nick that he knew him. He thought he was invisible in the crowd. Just another number.

Eidsvick's desk was a mess: a half-eaten bagel, piles of paper, red pens and paper clips. The office smelled old like dusty, antique books and the peeling eggshell-white walls made it feel older.

He stared at Nick over the rims of his glasses, twisting one of the thin pieces of metal between his fingers.

"Sir..."

"And don't give me any cockamamie line." He picked up the crescent of a cinnamon-raisin bagel and chomped down.

Nick had yet to determine where Dr. Eidsvick's odd accent originated. It could have been Scottish, Irish or any one of those ish's.

All he knew was the short, stocky Art History buff that wore a different bowtie for each day of the week was not from Georgia.

"I have heard it all. I do not like to waste my time, my breath and your parents' money. Why show up if you're not going to try?"

"It's taking some time to adjust. I thought things would be easier."

"Because it is art? Art is hard. Hard shit."

Nick figured his best move was to shut up and let him talk. Professors liked to talk—hear themselves talk, force you to listen to them talk, talk, talk.

Before he realized it, the professor's mouth moved— crusty pieces of bagel and cream cheese crowding the corners of his thin pink lips—but he heard no words.

"Hey, hey, you listening to me, kid?" He snapped his fingers and mumbled something in another language. "Why do I have office hours?"

"I'm listening."

"Yeah right. That's your problem Barclay. You zone out. I can tell it five rows away. It's in your eyes." He pointed two fingers at him and created circles in the stuffy air. "They glaze over like a hot, Krispy Kreme doughnut."

"I have a lot on my mind."

"You've got a lot on your mind, ha? That's a good thing. I began to wonder if anything was up there."

"I'm smart." Nick heard the defensiveness in his voice ring out. Honestly, he'd never felt so stupid his whole life. A couple months after high school graduation had rendered 12 years of As a completely useless accomplishment.

"Well, why don't you act like it? What do you like to do?"

"What do you mean?"

"Why are you in my class?"

His reason was commonsense but sounded too simple.

"I like to draw. Acrylic painting. Charcoal. I like...I love creating things."

"Hmmph. Is this what you want to do? Be an artist?"

Nick hunched his shoulders. He'd considered it, but starving artist seemed so unrealistic. There was no way he would be able to take care of himself and Lucille off a collection of sketches.

"I don't know. I haven't declared a major yet."

"It's no winning with you," Dr. Eidsvick grunted. "You make easy things hard, and the hard stuff you take it too easy."

"I'm still trying to figure everything out. It would really help me if I could do some extra credit work. I promise, I'll come to class. Listen. Take good notes. Whatever it takes."

He leaned back in his chair, hands behind his head, considering Nick's offer.

"Show me what you got, then."

Nick frowned. Everything this man said puzzled him. It was no wonder he was failing the class.

"Draw something. If it's any good, I'll see what I can do."

That was not the assignment he envisioned. He thought maybe he could write an extra essay or two, but this frightened him more than comma splices. Art was too subjective. Too personal.

"What, you're not happy with that solution?" he asked, pulling out a stack of essays.

Excuses abounded.

*I don't have any art supplies. I have no idea what to draw. How could this stuffy old man relate to anything I'd want to create?*

*Whatever it takes.*

"No, I can do it."

## Chapter Twenty Seven | *Nick*

During Nick's meeting with Eidsvick, the financial aid office left a voicemail letting him know his account had been flagged due to his GPA falling well below the range required by his HOPE scholarship.

A list of 'no's consumed him as he walked to the bus stop.

No HOPE, literally no hope. No money, no tuition, no class, no more AGU. No AGU = no life.

Back to Sandersville.

All signs were telling him that's where he belonged—that's where he was on the top of his game.

When the shuttle pulled up, Nick watched people crowd on but decided to go somewhere else.

He crossed Baker Street and walked down the steep hill to the raggedy corner building simply branded PACKAGE STORE in yellow block letters.

He found it funny how liquor was one of the only commodities that didn't require creative store marketing. The product sold itself effortlessly by existing.

Nick gave a homeless guy promising to tell a joke for 50 cents, $20 to buy him a bottle and keep the change.

He finished the bottle of vodka before the dark purple and orange splotches of sunset filled his room.

It numbed him to every single problem sprouting up like weeds in his life. Once he thought he solved one issue, something else popped up.

Nick passed out flat on his stomach, but felt like he was floating above all of it.

\* \* \*

"Hey babe."

Nick leaned back on the bench, pushing his foot against the cigarette receptacle, vanilla-scented smoke floated around him.

He woke up from his "nap" in the middle of the night and decided to walk it off. He ended up downtown, taking a couple more shots. When he ran out of cash, he knew it was time to head back to the Village. Still restless, he'd yet to make it up to his room.

The courtyard was empty, except for the occasional late night walk from one dorm to the other. The chirps of grasshoppers peppered the quiet night. The calmness reminded him of home, so he sat in it.

"You there?"

"It's three o'clock in the morning. What's wrong?" Jasmine's muffled words ran together in a sleepy haze.

"Nothing. Just thinking about life. How things just happen." He stared up at the big dipper dotting the coal-black sky, puffing out his own Black and Mild clouds.

"Are you drunk?"

"Maybe a little."

"Nick, you said you were going to stop."

"I know. This is it. I'm not going to get like this again. For real."

"What made you even think about drinking?"

"I don't know what I'm doing. It feels like nothing's going right. I just...I needed to chill out for a minute."

Jasmine yawned in the phone, but offered sincere support. "You've gotta focus, baby. It takes time to get used to something so major. What you're trying to do is a big deal."

"I don't belong here."

There was a long pause and he held his breath, letting the smoke flow through the alleyways of his nose.

"You wanna come home?"

"Yes, this ain't for me."

"You sure you want to do this? Why don't you sleep on it tonight and we can talk more in the morning?"

"Nah," he said, poking out his lips. "I can take a semester off and commute to Georgia College from home. I'll be close to you. And Grandma Lucille."

He shifted on the bench, taking in the Village, honing in on Roskill as if this really was goodbye.

"I see you have it all planned out."

"Yeah. Thought we might be able to get our own place together. Like you said."

She seemed instantly awakened.

"Aw, baby, that would be perfect. Daddy might not be fully on board with it at first, but he knows you're mature enough to take care of me. And that you love me."

The cigarillo tumbled from his fingers and while he heard Jasmine's voice, the words jumbled together in a fit of excitement.

In the shadows of his own despair and the darkness of 3 a.m. he recognized the couple pulling up in the turnaround.

The girl slammed the car door, which sounded extraordinarily loud in the dead of night. The guy rushed behind her, pulling her so hard she almost stumbled down the courtyard steps.

"Call me in the morning so we can talk about this some more. Okay? Love you," he whispered before Jasmine could say anything else.

He staggered closer, crushing red roses under his flip-flops, the sweet smell trailing him.

"No, no. Let me go," she shouted, the coils in her Afro flying in the light breeze. "Trey...if you don't let me go I swear I am going to scream."

He let go, but moved so close to her that from the distance it looked like he was either going to attack or give her a bear hug.

"Come here. Don't do this."

"I'm going to do it," she said.

"I love you and I know you love me too. We can make it work."

"*How*? Tell me how."

The silver light from the moon shone on the streams flowing down Maya's face. Trey kissed the wetness—each drop deliberately erased.

Nick couldn't hear the words he said to her as she gazed up at him, intoxicated, high in love with him.

He knew that look. Jasmine looked at him that way before she gave herself to him; the loyalty in her irises only deepened afterwards.

"Promise you won't," Trey demanded. "Promise me."

She didn't have to respond, her eyes wet and deep with fidelity.

Nick held up his phone and pressed record.

## Chapter Twenty Eight | *Ciara*

Professor Garrett strolled across the floor, clicker in hand, the slide showcasing *Freakonomics'* green apple with orange insides was large and bright in the dark classroom.

"So who wins the argument? Levitt or Gladwell? Was Roe v. Wade the real impetus for a decline in crime?"

His questions were met with the hum of the air conditioner. "I'll give an A for an answer. Any answer."

Even Laura Beth, the prim brunette overachiever who *always* raised her hand and *always* volunteered for team leader pretended to scribble down lecture notes.

"I guess it's time for a break. Come back with an answer or we might need an extra pop quiz before the final to ensure you guys are prepared."

Conversation of exhaustion bubbled immediately throughout the room. Freshman seminar was supposed to be the *easy* class, but Garrett made things so much harder with the pop quizzes, random readings and extra cultural outings.

"Part of me hopes he does give a quiz. Maybe Nick will finally learn his lesson and stop skipping," Faraji said.

Ciara stretched her long, lean body. "That's mean."

"I know. I haven't gotten through chapter four myself."

"It's a pretty good book. I mean, he brings up some interesting theories."

"Well, why didn't you answer his question?"

"You know me I like to keep it low-key."

"Girl, stop. You are always showing us up in this class."

"Honestly, I didn't get that far in the book yet. Besides I was sure Laura Beth's brown nose was going to be in the air."

"Say what you will about the girl. She helped me get an A on our group project," Faraji said.

"Whatever. She gave me an A+ headache." Ciara pulled out her debit and JavaWorks frequent customer discount cards from her leather wristlet.

"Go on and get your afternoon crack."

"It's the only thing that keeps me awake these days."

She took the classroom steps two at a time, not wanting to miss Garrett's potential quiz.

It was her fault that she'd failed to complete the assignment. She'd been watching out for Atlanta Braves Hat—who was either on vacation or had learned the art of discretion.

She'd also watched out for Trey. He hadn't returned her calls, texts, messages and notes she left on his door.

Maybe he'd gotten rid of him after all.

At this point, all she wanted was an honest explanation about what was happening between them. Why had he abandoned her? No matter what he needed her for, she was always there. When it was her turn, he was a no-show.

She approached the counter, but didn't bother to look at the chalkboard menu.

"Mocha Icy with an extra shot with only a little whipped cream?" asked Tammy, a smiling barista dressed in a khaki JavaWorks smock and matching visor.

"That's it. I guess I should think about switching up my order."

"Hey, if it works, it works."

She scribbled CC on the plastic cup, yelling the order to her partner Eli who began crushing ice.

"You're a little late today," Eli shouted over the grinding noise.

"The professor got carried away. He almost forgot to give us our break."

Her phone vibrated. Another text message from Tyler asking how her day was going. He really was a sweet guy. Almost too good to be true.

*I'm fine. How are you?* she thumbed.

One JW stamp away from a free drink and a sip of sweet, caffeinated heaven later, Ciara briskly moved through the hallway.

Sipping and responding 'yes' to Tyler's request for a date, she rounded the corner sharply.

As she wondered what it would be like to go out on a date with someone other than Trey, she collided into a hard body. Her whip cream smeared his red t-shirt and her cards tumbled to the floor.

"I am so sorry," she said, wiping away the white mess.

"I was looking for you anyway."

"Speak of the devil and he shall appear," she said, stooping to pick up her cards.

"What's that supposed to mean?"

She had so many questions, she didn't know where to start.

"Did you move and did your mom deactivate your cell phone?"

Trey held up both hands in a surrendering motion. She'd seen and heard this before.

"Like I said, I was looking for you. I've been trying to catch up with you, but we keep missing each other."

"Where were you last week? We had a plan. You were supposed to be there to scare him. Instead he had me cornered."

Ciara refused to cry. It was so weak. Life's ebb and flow had taken a toll, rendering her hypersensitive to the smallest thoughts.

She smelled the beer and cigarettes, felt his warm breath on her face...and the fear that made her more jittery than her caffeine addiction.

"I thought...I thought he was going to hurt me."

"Babe, I'm sorry for disappointing you again. I tried so hard."

"What happened?"

"Before I could get to you, I ran into your crazy ass girlfriend Safari or whatever started talking about having her guys beat me up."

"First of all her name is *Faraji*. And she's a good friend. Better than you've been."

"I showed up like I said I would. But those guys started coming towards me. And I can't screw up my future fighting with a bunch of football players over nothing."

"So you did come?" The relief in her voice gave him an opening.

"Yes. And I'm here now. Let's go get something to eat. Or you can come back to my room and we can talk this thing out."

"Talk what out? This doesn't change the fact that you left and have ignored me," she scoffed.

"I want to make things right. I promise. Whether we get back together or not. I owe it to you."

He peered right into the crack in the wall she was trying to build.

No matter what happened, she always had his heart and he hers.

"Come with me."

* * *

Ciara slid in one of the tan booths lining the side of JavaWorks.

"If it's so important, talk to me now."

"I'm going to be 100% honest with you." He clasped his hands on the center of the table.

Ciara slurped the remainder of her drink—a slush of caramel drizzle and whipped cream.

She wasn't sure she wanted the honest-to-God truth. Sure, that's what she said she wanted, but to sit across from him now, poised to deliver it, she was afraid.

"I heard about you and that guy. And I don't like it."

Ciara almost choked on the ice-cold, sugary mix. She thought about their night together and the messages that followed.

"Wait, what?" she coughed out. How did this sit-down turn into a discussion about her? Where was his apology?

"The football player that was threatening to kick my ass at the bar downtown?"

"What are you talking about?"

"Don't play the innocent role," he said, his voice rising. "You know you can't hide dirt in The Village. Nosy-ass desk assistants and RAs would tell me what time you peed this morning if I asked them."

"Oh."

"Yeah, *oh*. Why am I hearing about you getting drunk with this guy and then taking him up to your room? I know you *technically* broke up with me, but that was not an excuse to start wilding out."

"Wait, whoa, whoa, whoa. If you had been there, you wouldn't have to worry about anything happening with Tyler. And you do remember, you cheated on me right?"

He shook his head, his square jaw grinding. "I didn't cheat on you. I didn't."

"I caught you!"

"I danced with another girl, that's it."

Ciara tilted her head and gave him a 'Do you think I'm dumb?' look.

"What proof do you have that I ever cheated on you? Going to Miami for Spring Break with my homeboy and his lesbian friend?" he stopped, knowing that he was chipping away.

"Dancing on some girl I don't know at a dorm party? You put that together and decide to give up on two years. I thought we were better than this, CC."

"I don't know..." *whether I can trust you*, she finished the sentence in her mind.

He leaned forward. "You let a girl that you haven't known for a minute get in your head and convince you otherwise. She doesn't understand what we have."

"She was looking out for me."

"Ciara, babe, you have to learn how to stand on your own."

"I'm sorry." There was some truth in what he said. Her evidence was shaky and she didn't know Faraji that well. More than anything she wanted things to go back to how they were when it was just the two of them and none of these extra people crowding their relationship.

He pounded the table and both it and Ciara jumped. "I can't believe she set you up with some guy. And then you brought him to your room?"

Her eyes fell to her lap, guilt crawling through her nervous system.

It was his turn to ask what happened. His leg jumping up and down nervously, he repeated over and over again, "Tell me. I won't be mad."

He leaned back, speaking softer to coax her to where he wanted her to go.

"You've been through a lot with what happened with Tala. But I need to know the truth."

She wanted to tell him the same story she'd delivered to Faraji.

"Be honest."

She controlled her nose and looked straight ahead into the pool of his light brown eyes. "Nothing happened. I promise."

## Chapter Twenty Nine | *Nick*

"Babe, you were really gone."

Nick groaned, his voice guttural. "I know."

He pushed himself up in the bed with the heels of his feet. That slight movement had his world spinning on a crooked axis.

The pain was constant and so sharp he parted his eyes slowly. "I missed freshman seminar, again."

"What's going on to make you go back on your promise to stop drinking?" Jasmine asked. "I don't remember you getting like that ever in Sandersville."

"It won't happen again," he muttered. The aftermath and breaking Lucille's promise both made him want to throw up.

"When you come home everything will get better, sweetie."

"I still have to figure out my extra credit project. *And pray*," he laughed. "If I get an A, I'll be straight for the fall semester. Man I owe God so much after all the favors I've asked for."

The line filled with silence. Was she praying for him too? He needed all the prayer he could get at this point.

"Nick, you said you were coming home permanently."

"I told you that I was leaving?"

"Yes. That's what you said. That's *exactly* what you told me." His ear was extra sensitive to the soprano pitch of her voice.

That emotion within her was cancerous—abnormal and uncontrollable. It rushed out and she let it flow.

"You said you were going to be with me. And Miss Lucille."

"I was messed up last night. I don't even remember how I got to my room."

"You can't keep doing this to me. I can't let you string me along like this."

"I'm sorry, but I promise Jasmine I didn't mean to."

"If you tell me you're sorry one more time, I swear!" He held the phone away from his ear, unable to take the clash of pain in his eardrum. He stared at it, her soliloquy came through the speaker clear and strong.

"You're always sorry for something. But you never change. You do the same thing, over and over again. And I keep forgiving you."

He remained calm, pinching the bridge of his nose.

"I want to do better. You don't know how much I regret it all."

"How could I let you do this to me? We should have gone our separate ways. But no, I tried to *please you*. I wanted to do what made you happy. Forget my own happiness."

"If you'd let me say something."

"Why? So you can tell me more lies? I'm sick of it."

"Be quiet for a minute."

"I've been quiet too long. You can't stop me now. This is your fault. All because of you, I'm here in Sandersville by myself. Living with my parents. No job. No school. Thinking you'd be there for me."

He loved her and as much as he felt for her, these were not problems he had created.

She was the right one for him—*back then*.

She'd been perfectly the same. No change and no plan to ever change.

Was the plan to wait it out in Sandersville until he graduated and saved her?

"I don't wanna have to let you go. You were my first true love...ever," he said, talking over her. She was on a roll that the L word couldn't stop.

"I'm sorry."

He disconnected himself, pressing END to both the conversation and his relationship with Jasmine.

## Chapter Thirty | *Nick*

Nick was unavailable—emotionally, physically, spiritually and for whatever else anyone wanted from him.

He bribed Kenny to leave him alone for 24 hours straight, agreeing to allow him endless priority over the TV for the rest of the semester. Kenny made him promise he wasn't going to try anything crazy.

*Whatever it takes.*

In the quiet solitude of that room, no excuse kept him from not finishing the extra credit project. Getting Eidsvick's approval would solve his problems. He'd get his grade back up and maintain his scholarship.

Drawing usually calmed his nerves; the starting point was so easy when he became bored during class. Standing before this blank, white canvas and knowing what it meant to his future overwhelmed him.

He could do a sunset. There always was something magical about the natural way light and color came together at the end of the day.

That felt too cliché and he would have to wait ten hours for it to happen.

Nick pushed away the urge to walk to the liquor store for a bottle to get his creative juices flowing. Just a little taste to relax his nerves. Nothing extinguished his fears and inhibitions like a couple shots of vodka.

He had \$9.52 left in his checking account after buying the easel, canvas, paper and a cheap set of acrylic paint. With the minimum withdrawal set at \$20, he couldn't even get the cash from an ATM if he wanted to.

What was the perfect thing for him to present to Eidsvick?

He spent a couple hours flipping through his Art History textbooks and notes to see if Eidsvick favored a particular artist or period. None of it brought him any inspiration.

Nick looked around the room for potential pieces he could bring to life on the page.

He slid the brown trunk from under his loft. It opened with a creak. Amongst the stacks of miscellaneous items, from CDs, paperwork and DVDs and random books he uncovered a case of charcoals.

The black mineral was hard and cold between his fingers. Everything he needed had been there all along—soft, medium, hard pencils and compressed sticks.

A yellow note tumbled out of the case onto the floor. Folded over and over again, it was a tiny square. He smudged it with the black color on his fingertips.

*You have real talent that's going to make you famous one day. Love, Jasmine*

The note triggered something in him. A week later, the bruises from the break-up were still sore and he realized how much Jasmine intertwined with the DNA of his life. She had been part of him so long, he didn't know what it felt like to not have her. He imagined this was how people who lost limbs, but swore they were moving their arms felt.

He would see something happen on the street and want to text her "Can you believe this?" Or he would think of some idea, get excited and know that only she would get it.

Nick got on his knees, laid out a piece of paper.

"Please Lord." He didn't have the voice or strength to offer any more excuses.

Once the pencil touched down, it flowed. Lines, curves, shapes came together without him knowing what would happen next.

When he looked up five hours had passed by, his stomach growled and he had a woman's face before him.

It was as if he had fallen asleep, passed out and someone took over his body and created something beautiful. It did not seem possible for a D-student in Art History to design something like this.

*Who was she?*

He stepped back from her, tilted his head left, then right. Her intricate face was made up of little moments he saw in Jasmine's eyes (when she dreamed of love and marriage), Faraji's freckles (when she laughed at his lame jokes) and Ciara's lips (when she knew she had convinced someone she was right).

He had Frankenstein-ed the perfect woman.

It wasn't a typical portrait either. Her features popped off the page like a 3-D film. At the same time she was deeply connected to the world of various shapes and shades that kept her tethered to the page.

Nick had a long way to go. He needed to add some finishing touches to her body and her world. He wanted to do something dramatic, add color, lights and texture, because she deserved it.

## Chapter Thirty One | *Ciara*

"Spread your legs a little bit." He placed his palm against her thigh, let it stay there until she was where he wanted her to be. "That's it."

He gripped her waist tight, his fingers digging into her soft flesh. He eased her into position, ran his lips down the pulsating vein along her neck.

"Relax, relax," he whispered, his warm breath tickling her ear.

"I'm a little scared."

"Don't be. You ready?"

"I think so." She eased down, hesitating midway.

The pop of the .38 within the corridor was much louder than she expected, sending a flutter through her heart and a shiver down her spine. Ciara stumbled back into him and he caught her at her elbows.

"Wow."

The two videos the owner of Fire Away gun range forced them to watch beforehand hadn't prepared her for that moment after pulling the trigger.

"Felt good didn't it?" Trey asked, his lips curving up.

"I can't describe what it felt like."

"The power behind it is amazing." He massaged his fingers over the body of steel. "It's almost electrifying."

"You are a little excited about these guns. Should I be jealous?"

"Come on now."

"I'm just saying. You're rubbing really hard over there."

"When you have this in your hand, it doesn't matter who you're talking to. You're in charge."

She held the piece in her palm; it wasn't as heavy as she expected. "There's no doubt about that."

"Look, you almost got him in the head."

"Stop trying to make me feel better. That was nowhere near him."

"Ready to try again?"

Ciara adjusted the oversized headphones and safety glasses. She took a deep breath, closed her eyes, and imagined Atlanta Braves Hat, sneering at her.

His cold cerulean eyes held no pity or fear. She aimed for that space between them.

*BANG.*

\* \* \*

"When was the last time you saw him?"

She held the spoon of ice cream, meditating over his question before shoving the cookies and cream in her mouth.

"I think I saw him when I came over last night."

"He followed you to my room, the dorm, or what?"

"I could've sworn I saw him parked on the street when I was heading inside, but I don't think he followed me in. How could he? You have to have ID to get in."

Trey dipped his fry into a mix of ketchup and mayonnaise, looking around the crowded dining hall.

"I'm sure he could figure out how to get around that. I mean folks who aren't on the meal plan sneak up in here all the time."

"Don't say that. I need that false sense of security."

"Aw, babe, it's going to be alright. You are a regular old Lara Croft now."

"I don't know about that."

"With practice you'll get better. The point was to give you the confidence to defend yourself. To know that if the time comes, you'll have do whatever is necessary."

"Okay, Malcolm X. By any means necessary?"

"With some people you have to resort to things you never thought you'd do."

"I miss this," she said, squeezing his hands. "Us being together. No arguing. No fighting. No crazy accusations."

"Me too. You know how to make me relax and I needed this to take my mind off finals."

"Don't mention finals." She pulled out a deck of tattered, neon cards filled with notes and diagrams.

"I carry around this stack of note cards like it's my bible. I've got notes all over the place. I even used the mirror as a board."

"I love how when your heart is in something, you put in work."

"Lots of hard work."

"Wait until fall. It gets really real then."

"I don't think nothing could be worse than trying to cram five chapters in a day."

"It isn't the stuff happening inside the classroom you have to worry about. When August hits, there's something happening all the time."

"Oh, I can't wait for the step shows and football season," she said in a dreamy way. The summer session was like college lite—she was ready for the full experience. "You know I've never been to an AGU game?"

"It's something else. And there'll be ten Tylers trying to get at you," he chuckled.

She leaned in towards him. "I've worked too hard to keep you. Made too many sacrifices to lose you. Trust me."

## CHAPTER THIRTY TWO | *Nick*

Faraji shifted from under Nick as the credits rolled up his small TV.

They were high above it all on his lofted bed. Professor Garrett's final exam notes had been pushed to the side for a comedy break.

He waited for the perfect moment to present *The Perfect Woman* portrait to Faraji. Before he turned it in to Eidsvick, he wanted to get her blessing. He had written a few words to make sure he said everything he wanted to say, the right way.

*What if she doesn't get it? Or think it's junk?*

Faraji reached across him for the course companion, ready to get back to business.

He was nervous, unsure of how to keep her from reverting back to their purpose for meeting up.

"That same scene gets me every time. *Bang, bang, bang, bang!*" Nick mocked John Witherspoon's scene-stealing dinner table performance from the film *Boomerang*.

"That was hilarious." She laughed like she was watching the scene again.

"I'm trying to figure out how Eddie let Robin play him like that. He had so many man code violations."

"I like it how she flipped it on him. Men try to play the game, but when we do it, you can't handle it," Faraji said, shrugging.

"We have to protect our egos."

She faced him on the bed, crossing her legs. "Exhibit A. Trey didn't come sniffing around CC again until she kicked it with Tyler."

"Now they are different. She should never, ever, ever give him another chance."

Taken aback, she closed the book.

"So you've never had any drama like that in your past?"

"I'm not saying that. Dating and drama goes hand in hand."

"We don't have any drama. I mean that stunt you pulled the night we *you know*—we worked through that."

He was nodding his head up and down as if there were invisible headphones blasting in his ears. "But we're not *dating*. Are we?"

Faraji didn't say anything, but she became stiff, almost in a perfect yoga formation—minus the peace.

The question hadn't come out right. He cleared his throat. "You've been a real good friend since day one, so I just..."

She smiled, but he could tell she was vexed. "What are you trying to say?"

"There's something I probably should've told you sooner."

She stared at him without blinking, body still. "What? Stop playing around."

"I...wanted to let you know." He couldn't bring himself to say it. Not when her naturally brown eyes bore into him seeking truth.

How could he inflict the same pain he saw still clouding Lucille's storm-gray eyes? Or cause the internal scars that made Jasmine so needy?

Hurt women surrounded him and he'd done nothing to ease their pain. If anything, he exacerbated it.

"What I should have told you was…"

"About your little girlfriend? You damn right you should've told me."

The white, lemon meringue ceiling closed down on him. His tongue fell flat in his mouth, eyes roamed downwards following the creases in the sheet crumpled against her thigh.

"Don't try to deny it," she said softly.

"Faraji, please."

"Please, what? Please tell the truth for once!"

"You don't have the full story."

She leaned against the wall plastered with a black and white poster of Muhammad Ali hovering like a killer bee over Sonny Liston.

"So a few days ago, I was talking with Scarlett at the front desk. You know we're pretty cool," she said, linking her hands as a symbol of their solidarity. "And she was telling me about how some crazy chick came looking for you. How she was your girlfriend from Sandersville?"

"At the time we were sort of in an open situation."

"An open situation? Sort of?" Faraji asked, incredulously. "What is that supposed to mean?"

"We were...well I was open to see other people."

"She *let* you see other women?" She mouthed *Wow*.

He sat silently, letting it soak in.

Was there any point in telling her that he was done with Jasmine?

"Why didn't you say anything?" he asked.

"At first I was pissed. We were friends."

The finality of *were* stung him.

"I felt like I'd played myself."

"No, I wanted to be with you, Faraji. I *choose* to be with you."

"And then I was relieved," she interrupted, speaking over him.

"*Relieved?*"

"Remember the night we went to Garrett's? And I was acting funny?"

"Yeah, you were mad because I left you. But I explained to you about CC."

"Deep down inside, I regretted what happened. You started texting me all the time. It seemed like you wanted something more. The thought of being tied down by another relationship so soon—it scared me."

She palmed his face with her hand, ran her fingers down his neck, over his broad shoulder, resting over his left ventricle pumping erratically.

"I thought I was going to have to break your heart. But *thank God* you screwed up and lied."

Faraji gathered her books, notes and climbed down.

"You don't have to leave. She and I broke up."

She stopped at the door and he thought he saw his chance. She couldn't have meant what she'd said. "It doesn't matter, Nick. I can't trust you as a friend or anything else."

## Chapter Thirty Three | *Ciara*

Ciara read the letter again. The thrill of the Fall semester ahead surged through her. She was anxious to close this chapter in life and move on.

"Ivylize," she repeated the name of her new roommate. "Preferred name: Ivy. Drama major. Interesting."

When she initially went through the residence hall selection process, she was disappointed they didn't have any private rooms available. She couldn't fathom life in a room the size of a prison cell with a complete stranger.

But the loneliness of summer left her feeling like she'd missed out on something.

She'd never shared a pizza with Tala. Never got to borrow her nail polish or watch reality TV over popcorn. No late night chats about boyfriends or upcoming dates.

But this would all change next month. She reached for her phone. She couldn't wait to talk about who would provide what and get to know Ivy.

The face of her phone lit up, the clock large and bright: 9:37 a.m. It was too early, especially on a Saturday.

Ciara mapped out the rest of her day dedicated to preparing for her sociology final, refusing to wake up at 3 a.m. again, drooling on her laptop track pad.

The tap on her door was so soft, she almost missed it. It came back again. This time three confident knocks. Upon opening it, she wished she'd checked the peephole first.

"What are you doing here?"

"There's something I need to tell you."

Ciara didn't realize how tight she was squeezing the doorknob until the sharp pain began to burn her wrist.

"Are you going to let me in or what?"

She stood still, the pangs increasing with her grip. She focused on it to help prepare for the blow her visitor was about to deliver.

"I asked you a question." Ciara's rage echoed against the walls of the hallway. She didn't care if her nosy neighbors heard and came out as they often did whenever signs of drama erupted in the dorm.

"Look," Maya began, pushing a ringlet with her index finger. "I don't know what Trey told you about me and him, but I'm here to tell you the truth, okay?"

"Your version of the truth?"

"The real, unadulterated truth. If you don't want it, I don't have to give it to you. I'm not dealing with him ever again."

The two stood there, emotional mirrors of each other. Tight, gray AGU shorts hugged her voluptuous hips and the white tee spread so thin across her chest that Ciara could see her leopard print bra.

*I can't believe she is standing here at my door telling lies.*

*You are lying to yourself. Yes you can.*

*She seduced him.*

*He's been lying to you since day one. You know she's not gay.*

*She could be gay. Or bi.*

*Or just plain trifling.*

Impatient with the invisible debate roaring between Ciara's heart and mind, Maya snapped her fingers, her neon yellow and pink acrylic nails clicking.

"I didn't have to come here."

"No, you didn't," Ciara said, folding her arms. "And you shouldn't have."

"I felt bad, you know. I thought..."

"You're not the first girl to try to take my boyfriend away from me."

Maya scoffed, lowering her chin. "Are you serious?"

"He loves me. Now, I don't know what sort of fling you had with him down in Miami and tried to rekindle, but accept that your tricks didn't work."

Ciara wanted to hurt her. She felt the burning ascension of anger that had risen when she saw the Muppet-faced girl dancing with Trey. She wanted to make Maya feel less than and know that she would never be on her level.

"Why would he want to be with someone like you?"

Maya simmered at the insult, her thick lashes fluttering, then she cackled.

"You don't have to worry about me anymore. In fact, you never had to worry about me." She bit the inside of her jaw— one pain distracted her from the other.

"I thought he wanted to be with me."

Ciara glimpsed surrender and the taste of victory.

"The reason I came over here was to tell you about..." Maya paused and pulled a stack of papers from her brown leather bag. "Some girl named, FierceChickXOXO?" She tossed the thick roll and Ciara caught it.

"I knew he was going to break up with you sooner or later." She flitted her hand in the air as if Ciara's status of girlfriend meant absolutely nothing.

"Anyway. To find out all along he had been with some other female too? That didn't sit right with me. It pissed me off actually. I wanted to beat the..."

Ciara was so engrossed in reading the salacious conversations printed in black and white, Maya's voice and words clashed together like underwater garble.

"...I'm just saying, if that's what they talked about online, can you imagine what they actually did? And this dummy leaves his inbox up and tries to act like it was his roommate's account. I know his username. And then she had it all out there for the world to see the whole time. That dirty bastard."

Ciara slowly closed the door on Maya and her verbal journey seeking closure. It was something she needed to secure too. But where would she begin? How could she find truth when it had been covered by so many lies? Lies Trey had spouted. Lies she had told herself.

"Hey are you okay?" Maya knocked, but Ciara refused to open the door.

The hard lump in the back of her throat refused to go down and she couldn't respond.

Her hands were shaking so badly, the paper sliced her finger. The redness spread quickly over the passionate words Trey wrote to someone else:

**@FierceChickXOXO** *U have no idea how bad I want you. Ur mine.*

She knew exactly who FierceChickXOXO was and called him.

"We need to talk."

## Chapter Thirty Four | *Nick*

He watched the sun creep closer to the edges of the canopy of magnolia trees.

The day, over and done with, left him restless.

Nick poured every fiber of his heart and soul in *The Perfect Woman*, but Eidsvick had yet to tell him if he was getting full credit for the project. He had failed to show it to Faraji to get her opinion and that injection of confidence—like Jasmine usually gave him.

It was funny how *The Perfect Woman* had been so valuable to him when he first created her, but with each rejection, she was almost worthless at this point.

He sat at his desk, rotating left to right in the computer chair. He caught her looking at him out the corner of his eye. It could have been his imagination, but her eyes looked sadder.

Maybe he should have created a sunset. A bowl of fruit. Some blond-haired girl with a hula-hoop on her foot?

Maybe what he'd created was crap. But what if it was meant to be amazing?

The uncertainty consumed him. He could use a little something in his drink—just a splash to settle his nerves, not enough to get drunk.

"Is tonight a full moon?"

"No. Why?" Kenny asked, his chubby fingers pressed against his double chin. The blue-fire lit computer screen reflected on his glasses.

"Does vodka turn you into a werewolf or something?"

Nick took a slow slip from his cup.

"It's just juice. I've learned my limits."

"Yeah, right. And I am dating Carmen," Kenny said. He laughed and his stomach jiggled so hard it looked like the image of Peter Griffin on his blue t-shirt was giggling too.

"I'm serious, man. I made some of the worst decisions and phone calls every single time I drank."

He scrolled and clicked. "Yeah well, we all have regrets. Alcohol induced or not."

"What's your biggest regret?" Nick asked.

"This semester? I mean you gotta be specific."

"Okay, this summer."

"Stalking Carmen," he mumbled. Nick noticed that his face didn't become full with pink this time. "Ever since I met her on the bus, I was nearly obsessed with her."

"Nah, you weren't near, you were."

"That's possible. Then I found out she had a crazy-face boyfriend. I mean this guy's got to be a methhead or on blow or something. His face is screwed up. He's got demon tattoos all over. And he's always starting fights downtown."

"You know all this about him how?"

"Her profile. She posts everything. This dude punched a bartender in the face because she messed up a drink order. Yes, *she*."

"He sounds nothing like you."

"Exactly! Part of me wishes I would've stepped up and said something. Showed her a different kind of guy."

"That's pretty emo, Kenny G."

"You asked. I answered."

"Yeah, you always keep it 100. Even if you know I'm gonna go in on you for it."

He mimicked a three-pointer and tossed the empty cup towards the trashcan. It bounced against the edge and rolled on the floor near her: his odd, red, black and white portrait of desire incarnate.

Why did he hide her?

Nick pulled on a wrinkled Main Street Bookstore t-shirt over his black Jordan basketball shorts. He eased the canvas out of the corner, faced her and a warm feeling of pride swelled within him. Whether Eidsvick gave him the A, he didn't care. He loved everything about her. She made him smile and feel happier than he'd been a long time.

Kenny scrunched his nose. "Are you alright bro? Where're you headed so fast?"

"To fix some regrets."

## Chapter Thirty Five | *Nick*

He jogged across the courtyard, up the steps to Caldwell, holding *The Perfect Woman* close to his side–not ready to share her and risk a negative comment on her strange beauty.

The silver elevator doors slid open and a big group dressed for a night out came off. Their laughter and smiles reminded him of how he felt when AGU was new and fresh.

Nick prayed that he wasn't about to spoil that experience for someone else.

The hall appeared longer than usual. He passed girls getting ready for bed, towels wrapped around their bodies and head. He wasn't sure if they looked at him funny or the anticipation of being so close to Faraji made him nervous with paranoia.

Nick wanted to ask for her forgiveness and friendship again, but it was too early. She told him she needed time, so he gave her the space. Still he couldn't let the semester end without her knowing how much she meant to him.

He could hear the television blasting some sitcom and shrill laughter at each punch line. The door was crowded with pink and purple paper balloons, streamers and birthday decorations for Faraji's roommate Katie.

Cuddling *The Perfect Woman* in his arm, he slid out the dry-erase marker. He held the cap in his mouth, writing 'I hope you like it. Nick' in neat purple letters.

He laid the canvas against the door, facing outwards, giving her the freedom to watch all who passed by like Mona Lisa would. Free for all to soak in her light and beauty.

Nick couldn't stop looking back. It was more than a picture—she was part of him too.

The elevator came quickly and there was only one other person on.

"Looks like I'm goin' same place as you," Nick said, seeing that Ciara's floor number was lit.

The man didn't respond, staring straight ahead.

Nick tried not to stare at his tapered Wranglers, clunky white Reeboks and slightly cocked Atlanta Braves hat.

He rehearsed how he would approach Ciara, but each version sounded harsh in his mind. After finding out that she had gotten back with Trey, he felt that she needed to know the truth. He pulled out his cell, ready to show her the evidence when she questioned whether he was being honest.

The elevator dinged and the man went to the left, Nick headed right towards the West wing.

He lifted his hand to knock on Ciara's door, but the deep voice behind it halted him. He pushed his ear against the wood.

The same voice. The same words. Just a different girl.

"I love you and I know you love me too. We can make it work."

CHAPTER THIRTY SIX | *Ciara*

He cried. In the lifetime that Ciara had known him, she'd never seen Trey cry.

She took a step forward, wishing she could redo all the moments that brought them to this scary place. She wanted to erase all the lies that flipped their plan of a lifetime together on its head.

She wanted to tell him everything would be fine, but that too was a lie.

"Will you forgive me?" he asked before admitting to any guilt.

Ciara held the papers. Like one of her favorite romance novels, the edges were wrinkled from re-reading the words, dissecting everything Trey's other woman said.

The schizophrenic stream of messages had smiley faces and virtual shout-outs to her followers that were as lively as they were macabre.

She shared what she ate.

Every show she watched.

Her heartbreak.

Her obsession between each line made Ciara shiver. She looked through Trey, towards Tala's empty side of the room. She imagined them tussling in the sheets. Her modeling hooker heels. Him kissing her neck as she gushed about every waking moment of their affair.

Tala was long gone and yet still there alive and in love online.

It began with one message over a year ago—an impressionable local girl met a charismatic college guy.

*FierceChickXOXO: met a nice college dude today...think i'm n luv already :D*

From that moment on, she showed how love could be a self-inflicted disease that attacked the heart first, then the mind and eventually souls.

Ciara had highlighted the messages that told a hidden side of her own story—the side that hurt her more than anything.

*FierceChickXOXO: dad would kill me if he knew...sure of it. For now, it's our little secret.*

*FierceChickXOXO: Errytime Is Like the 1ˢᵗ Time xoxo*

*FierceChickXOXO: thinkin about someone special...I wish he was here \*sigh\**

*FierceChickXOXO: stayed in his bed all day...could get used 2 this :) xoxo*

*FierceChickXOXO: bought some HAUTE new shoes for my babes check em out xoxo*

*FierceChickXOXO: he told me i am his and he is mine... #itstrue xoxo*

*FierceChickXOXO: he makes me do things id never do for nebody...YUUP! xoxo*

*FierceChickXOXO: some things and people are worth the wait #quote #love*

*FierceChickXOXO: Saw her @ orientation today. Let's just say me > her*

*FierceChickXOXO: hes with me 2night...right now xoxo*

*FierceChickXOXO: i wonder does she know...lol xoxo*

*FierceChickXOXO: on the sideline>>>> this sux xoxo*

*FierceChickXOXO: I HATE HER.*

*FierceChickXOXO: My life feels like hell without him. I'm gonna make hers feel like hell with him.*

*FierceChickXOXO: People will mistreat u if u let them. Sometimes u have to do something drastic to let them know ur serious*

*FierceChickXOXO: ya'll i finished a whole bottle of wine by myself*

*FierceChickXOXO: tired of it all...*

*FierceChickXOXO: @TheRealTreyYuup on top of the world...literally, u kno where. Our spot. xoxo*

*FierceChickXOXO: @TheRealTreyYuup only u can save me*

*FierceChickXOXO: if i fall will u catch me...hmm*

*FierceChickXOXO: signing off XOXO*

His voice brought her from the demented words that she read in Tala's voice.

"I'm telling you she was crazy. Had been stalking me since she found out about you. Did you know she *requested* you as a roommate?"

Ciara shook her head.

How had the police missed these messages? Trey and Tala's relationship? These were such critical pieces of evidence. Mr. Bing was right. The "investigators" weren't doing their job at all. And in all their do-nothing, they had left her out to dry and Mr. Bing in the dark.

Trey stretched out his hands and pulled her close to him. "I know I should have told you, but I was scared I'd lose you forever. I made a mistake, I know. But I love you more than anything, and she wanted to drive us apart."

"Were you with her that night?"

"What are you talking about? You picked me up, remember?"

"Before you went downtown. Were you with Tala?"

Three quick taps against the door stole their attention.

"Ciara, you in there?"

"Who is that?" Trey asked, his thick brows knitting together.

"I have no idea. I wasn't expecting anybody."

"What did you do?"

"I didn't do anything."

"Are you trying to set me up?"

"No. Why are you so paranoid?" She raised her bare toes on their tips to peek through the peephole. "It's Nick."

She began to untwist the lock.

"Don't even think about opening that door."

His tone made her pause. She didn't want to turn around, afraid of what she might see.

She felt it. The click of the safety confirmed it.

"CC, it's me Nick! I stopped by to, um, get those notes for the final."

Her hands were unsteady like her voice. "If I don't open it, he's going to think something is wrong."

"I don't give a damn. Until we straighten this out."

He held the gun at his side, aimed at the floor. But she'd seen his passion and precision at the gun range.

"What did Maya tell you?"

"She doesn't even know it's Tala. I wanted to confront you because I thought you'd finally tell me the truth."

"Ciara! I know you're in there." The distraction of Nick's voice booming through the door made him flail the gun towards her.

"Don't," she pleaded, cowering. "Trey, don't do this."

"Why won't you forgive me?"

She breathed heavily, thinking, willing her body to stop shaking, praying for the right words to say.

"Don't I always? What makes you think this time is going to be any different?"

He wiped away the sweat mingling with tears from his face with his arm. "I didn't kill her."

"You'd never do something like that."

"No. I can't. I can't go to jail."

"You won't. Put the gun away and I'll forgive you."

"She wanted to jump," Trey whispered.

"I know. She was sick, baby."

"She tried to take me with her. She wanted to destroy *us*."

He clenched his free hand into a fist, holding on to something. "I just...I let her fall."

Trey wasn't there anymore. Eyes glazed over, he was on that rooftop, describing the night as it had happened.

"She was so drunk. Wanted to know if I could live without her. Started talking crazy about calling you. About *killing* you because I didn't want to be with her."

"You did it for me?"

"She slipped. I tried to help, but she kept shouting at me. I couldn't think. I had to...just let her go."

Ciara moved towards him. She fought through her words. "I forgive you." Palmed his cheeks between her hands. "I love you."

He folded his arms around her and inhaled her scent—a seductive blend of fear, adrenaline and rose-scented perfume.

"I love you too. I did it for us."

## Chapter Thirty Seven | *Nick*

Nick stood on the other side of the door. The quietness scared him more than anything. Trey and Ciara had gone from shouting to silence. He only heard his own labored breathing.

*What's going on in there?*

He bent down on the thin carpet; closed one eye to get a good view through the narrow slice. He saw her bare feet and his shoes so close together.

As he began to get up he noticed Reeboks. And then tight Wranglers. Beer belly. Atlanta Braves Hat.

"What the hell are you doing here?"

"I could ask you the same question," Nick said, frowning.

The man removed the toothpick, looked from the top of the door to the carpet.

"I don't have time for this," he grunted.

Nick wasn't sure if he was talking to him the way the man glanced down at the phone in his hand.

"I don't know what's going on, but that's my friend in there and she—"

In one swift motion he turned his back to the door and slammed his heavy Reeboks against the doorjamb. Three UFC-worthy kicks splintered the wood.

He rushed Trey, tackling him to the cold, hard floor. He hit him so hard the blow crushed his jaw. Blood gushed out the corner of his mouth, crimson trickling onto the soft crème rug near the futon.

Trey struggled to breathe under the man's weight as he twisted his arms.

"I sure do appreciate that confession," he said in Trey's ear. "I can't arrest you, but you're goin' to jail. Tonight."

Trey's eyes ran wildly across the room and he tried to talk, but it came out baby-babble.

Ciara rushed towards him. "Nick. Nick. Oh my God. Nick."

"It's okay." He rubbed her back, enveloping her in his arms. "You scared me."

"I didn't know what I was doing."

"Clearly trying to be a superhero," he said.

She trembled, her eyes locked on Trey's. The enduring connection between the two of them made Nick shudder.

"And who is this Stone Cold Steve Austin wannabe?"

"Somebody who knew where the truth was all along," she sniffled.

"I just needed him to slip up and tell the truth to the right person," he said. "Couldn't've done it without you Miss Capers. Glad you gave me that call."

That was her cue to celebrate her good deed, but Nick could tell that the justice being served did not calm her soul.

"How could you leave her?" she asked, staring down at Trey. "You let her fall and then you went out for a good time? You used me as an alibi."

He offered no answer or apology, just laid there silently refusing to make eye contact.

Ciara winced at the injury invisible to the eye and buried her face in Nick's chest.

Red, white and blue flashing lights filled The Village courtyard, filtering in through the blinds.

A few students eyed the police cars suspiciously. They lingered in the lobby and slowed their late night strolls.

This time they knew it wasn't a random fire drill. Monday was the last day of summer session after all.

Most were morbidly curious, watching every move.

They observed conversations between the investigators and residents.

Just like that night.

Thank you so much for reading! The story definitely doesn't stop here. This began as a single story almost 10 years ago when I was an undergraduate.

But I had a problem. There were just too many characters and too many topics and story lines that I wanted to cover.

The Village Series is meant to capture the college experience at a major division I institution, particularly from the eyes of African American students. I remember experiencing a bit of culture shock my freshman year and I had to overcome many challenges (internal and external) as a 'minority.'

I always thought it was just me and that perhaps I was sensitive. Then I talked to other alumni and realized they had similar experiences, if not worse. I hope that I showed some of this in a way that lets others know that it's not just you. You are not alone and it's so important to seek opportunities and communities that will welcome you.

This writing and publishing journey has truly been a labor fueled by love and support from many friends and family members.

I'm so thankful to God for blessing me with the talent, experiences, people, endurance and faith to take this step. I also must recognize my family for keeping me lifted: Betty Poole for waiting and aggravating me about this for 20 years; Charlie Poole, Jr. for introducing me to the art of storytelling; Ty Poole for inspiring me to finish with unsolicited advice that only a child would give; Charles Poole for encouraging me to go after what I want; and Fred Hurt for always being so supportive and positive.

And last but not least my friends and readers—your encouragement, feedback and comments throughout the YEARS brought this novella to life. I hope it made you proud. We did that!

With all my love,
Lakeshia

**Read excerpts from the next installation and more fiction at www.LakeshiaPoole.com**

**Follow me at Twitter.com/JustLakeshia and Facebook.com/LakeshiaPooleWrites.**

37095906R00131

Made in the USA
Charleston, SC
27 December 2014